BOOKS BY ELIZABETH EULBERG

The Great Shelby Holmes
The Great Shelby Holmes Meets Her Match

⌐•THE GREAT•¬
SHELBY HOLMES

ELIZABETH EULBERG

illustrated by ERWIN MADRID

BLOOMSBURY

NEW YORK LONDON OXFORD NEW DELHI SYDNEY

First published in the United States of America in September 2016
by Bloomsbury Children's Books
Paperback edition published in September 2017
www.bloomsbury.com

Bloomsbury is a registered trademark of Bloomsbury Publishing Plc

For information about permission to reproduce selections from this book, write to
Permissions, Bloomsbury Children's Books, 1385 Broadway, New York, New York 10018
Bloomsbury books may be purchased for business or promotional use. For information on
bulk purchases please contact Macmillan Corporate and Premium Sales Department at
specialmarkets@macmillan.com

The Library of Congress has cataloged the hardcover edition as follows:
Names: Eulberg, Elizabeth, author.
Title: The Great Shelby Holmes / by Elizabeth Eulberg.
Description: New York : Bloomsbury, 2016.
Summary: Nine-year-old Shelby Holmes, the best detective in her
Harlem neighborhood, and her new easy-going friend from downstairs,
eleven-year-old John Watson, become partners in a dog-napping case.
Identifiers: LCCN 2015040010
ISBN 978-1-68119-051-8 (hardcover) • ISBN 978-1-68119-052-5 (e-book)
Subjects: | CYAC: Mystery and detective stories. | Friendship—Fiction. |
Harlem (New York, N.Y.)—Fiction.
Classification: LCC PZ7.E8685 Gr 2016 | DDC [Fic]—dc23
LC record available at https://lccn.loc.gov/2015040010

ISBN 978-1-68119-053-2 (paperback)

Book design by Jessie Gang
Typeset by RefineCatch Limited, Bungay, Suffolk
Printed and bound in the U.S.A. by Berryville Graphics Inc., Berryville, Virginia
2 4 6 8 10 9 7 5 3 1

All papers used by Bloomsbury Publishing, Inc., are natural, recyclable products
made from wood grown in well-managed forests. The manufacturing processes
conform to the environmental regulations of the country of origin.

For my fabulous agent, Erin Malone,
who has Watson's heart and Shelby's smarts
(and sometimes her mouth!), for your
excitement and enthusiasm since day one

↶·CHAPTER·↷

1

EVERY WRITER NEEDS A GOOD STORY TO TELL.

So here was my problem: I had nothing to write about because nothing exciting had ever happened to me. Seriously, nothing. Zip. Zilch. Nada. Diddly-squat. You'd think that someone who grew up on four different army posts in eleven years would've witnessed *at least one* exciting thing. Yeah, you'd think.

Nope.

My life = boring.

Then we moved from Maryland to New York City, and my new neighbor tried to blow up the building.

Sure, it all started like your average moving day for the Watson family. I'd gotten used to the constant packing and unpacking that came with having a mom in the military. But this time was supposed to be different. Mom and I were going to settle here, in an apartment at 221 Baker Street. We were even flattening out the boxes and leaving them outside by the curb, instead of saving them for the inevitable future move.

Oh, and this was also the first time we were moving without Dad. As much as a writer needed to tell the whole story, I wasn't ready to go there. Yet.

So yeah, it was your typical moving day. Or so it seemed. It figured that the moment Mom became a civilian and we were off the military post and *allegedly* safe, we found ourselves dodging an explosion.

BOOM!

Our entire apartment shook. Mom grabbed me and pulled me down to the floor, covering my head. The four bulky movers attempted to seek shelter behind our furniture.

The only person who wasn't ducking for cover was our new landlady, Mrs. Hudson.

"Oh heavens!" she exclaimed with a shake of her head. "No need to panic, everybody! It's really nothing." She excused herself, muttering "I told her not today" under her breath.

Maybe explosions were a routine occurrence in this apartment building? If that was the case, I'd take the army post any day over some crazy New Yorker with a stick of dynamite.

The building was eerily silent for a few minutes, and we all returned to the business of moving and unpacking boxes.

Mom gave me an uneasy smile. "Well, John, it looks as if you finally have something exciting to write about in your journal."

Yeah, though I could've done without the stress of thinking we'd been bombed. For some reason, my grandma insisted on giving me a journal for my birthday every year. They were half-filled with unfinished stories of space travel and doodles of my unoriginal comic book characters: Awesome Dude, Tarantula Man, Sergeant Speedo, and Amazing Girl.

I stuck to fiction since there wasn't a reason to journal about my real life. Because my life was boring, dull, uninteresting, lackluster, monotonous, unexciting. (Grandma had also given me a thesaurus.)

I guess you could think that moving to a new place was exciting, but it was something we did so often that it was more of a pain. And it was hard. New friends, new teachers, new routine. Once I got all that down, the days on post would always run together: school, playground, homework, and bedtime. Repeat. Then we'd move and it would start all over again. It didn't matter if I was in Georgia, Kentucky, Texas, or Maryland. Somehow, it was always the same.

All that was about to change.

"Sorry!" Mrs. Hudson reentered our apartment, pulling someone behind her. "You know what to do," she ordered through clenched teeth.

A skinny white girl with bright red frizzy hair came forward. She had on an oversized white lab coat and goggles pushed up on her forehead. From the waist up, she was covered with black soot, except for where her goggles had been. She placed a hand on her hip. "I've been informed by Mrs. Hudson that my *harmless and perfectly safe* experiment has made for an unpleasant moving day for you. I've been instructed to apologize." She sighed heavily.

Ah, did she consider that *an apology?*

"Thanks, dear. Do you live in the building?" Mom asked, always in a rush to make friends for me whenever we got to a new place (mostly out of guilt, since she was the reason we had to move so much). But this girl, who looked to be no older than seven, was way too young for me to hang out with. I just turned *eleven*. I didn't need to spend the rest of my summer babysitting. *Especially* some weird science geek.

"Yes. Upstairs in 221B." The girl walked over to Mom and extended her hand to shake. "How long were you in Afghanistan?" she asked.

My mom's arm paused in midair as she glanced over at me. We were both thinking the same thing.

How did she know that?

The girl continued, "You're an army doctor, I presume? And by the way you favor your right leg, it appears that you injured your left side somehow. Hip? I hear shrapnel can be quite painful."

This was strange on so many levels. Mostly because whenever my mom's military service and injury were brought up, people avoided eye contact and spoke in a hushed voice. Not this girl. Nope. It was like she was asking about the weather. Her tone was even while her gaze mostly remained on Mom, but occasionally her attention would switch gears as if she was looking for something.

Mom's jaw was practically on the floor. "How did you—"

She was cut off by the sound of broken glass coming from the living room.

Awesome. Moving day kept getting better and better.

One of the movers removed a blanket that had been protecting a floor-length mirror.

"This wasn't wrapped up tightly

enough." The guy shrugged and continued to unwrap the blanket. "Couldn't be helped."

"Stop!" the girl shouted at him. She strode over and examined the broken glass.

Mrs. Hudson laughed lightly to break the tension. "Oh, it's just this thing she does."

Um, okay. As if *that* explained what was going on. Were all New York City kids like that?

"Hey!" the mover yelled at her. "What are you doing?"

The girl was on her hands and knees, her face mere inches from the guy's feet. Quickly, she jumped up and wiped her hands. "He kicked the mirror in."

"I didn't—" the mover began to protest.

She pointed to his shoe. "Based on the angle of the hole in the mirror, which is the size of the toe of your boot, the hole occurred at an upward trajectory, an angle that matches the height of our front steps. Therefore, I've correctly deduced that you did indeed kick the mirror while walking up the steps. While in all probability said event was an accident, it certainly was your fault."

The only thing clear to me was that I now lived among bombers and freaks.

"Would you care for me to draw a diagram, or are you going to save us all time and confess?" The mover stood there, dumbstruck. The rest of us were shocked as well.

Except for Mrs. Hudson, who seemed amused and a little bit tired.

The mover stuttered for a few moments before bending down so he was eye-to-eye with the girl. "Who *are* you?"

Her lips curled upward into a satisfied smile. "I'm Shelby Holmes. *Detective* Shelby Holmes."

CHAPTER
2

SINCE I WAS SICK OF UNPACKING I DECIDED TO SPEND THE next morning outside, on the steps of our new home—a brownstone building in Harlem, which is way on the upper, upper west side of Manhattan. Mom was busy with meetings at her new job at the Columbia University Medical Center. She gave me permission to explore the neighborhood, as long as I was careful and remained in a ten-block radius of our building.

Careful? I'd rather take my chances on the streets of Manhattan than be stuck inside an apartment building with some girl who liked to set off explosives.

As much as I wanted to walk around my new neighborhood and maybe also meet some people who weren't trying to kill me, I was a little overwhelmed. New York City was very different from anywhere else we'd lived. On the army posts, we were relatively contained. Now the possibilities were endless. I had no idea where to start. Did I head east?

Or west? Or uptown? Or downtown? And which way was east? Or west?

Instead, I settled in with my journal. Yeah, it was old-school that I favored pen and paper over a computer. But there was something, I don't know, more personal about writing a story out with your hand instead of tapping at a keyboard.

Not like I'd done a lot of writing lately.

I hadn't written anything in months. I'd tried, but I just couldn't do it. It was pretty ironic that when things were actually happening in my life, I froze.

But now . . . I suddenly had an itch to write. I looked at the blank pages, trying to find some way to describe what happened yesterday. How did this little girl know all that stuff about Mom? And the mover? I was fascinated, but also really, really creeped out.

I considered myself lucky she hadn't turned her attention toward me.

Just then, the front door opened and shut with a bang. Without even turning my head, I knew my luck had run out.

Shelby skipped down the steps, leading a white-and-brown English bulldog on a leash.

"John Watson"—she nodded at me—"meet Sir Arthur."

I reached down and petted the dog, who slumped happily and rolled over so I could rub his belly.

Great. The only living creature to welcome me to town was a slobbering dog.

"Sir Arthur?"

"Well, he *is* British," she remarked. "And the best dog ever. Since the Queen hasn't seen fit to reply to my correspondence about making such an extraordinary animal an official member of the Order of the British Empire, I've taken it upon myself to honor him with the designation of respect he deserves and call him 'Sir.'"

That dictionary Grandma had also given me was going to get some serious use if I kept talking to Shelby Holmes.

She bent down to give him a quick belly rub. "Well, we've got our rounds to make. Come on!"

The dog rose reluctantly and continued down the stairs.

"Wait!" I called out, surprising myself. Before I could really think things through, I decided to go for broke. "Can I come with you?"

Yeah, she was strange. But I had to find out how she'd done all that stuff yesterday. Okay, and I was a little intimidated to walk around the neighborhood by myself. Not like a tiny girl could do much to defend me, but at least we had Sir Arthur.

Shelby shrugged indifferently. "Suit yourself."

As we walked down our street, lined with brownstones that matched our own building, Shelby launched into a detailed explanation of her "rounds." Honestly, I could only follow part of what she said. She talked really fast and was rattling off a long list of people she always checked in with daily.

I did, however, understand one thing: Shelby Holmes was a very nosy girl.

I started to count the blocks as Shelby turned onto Lenox Avenue (that's one block away from home). I was surprised by all the taxis and cars that whizzed by. There were so many things to take in: the noise, the stores with signs in foreign languages, the people, the different outfits (one guy had on colorful silk pajamas and a matching hat), and the crowds as we crossed 125th Street (now we were five blocks away from home, or was it six?).

I nodded at a guy who was selling hats at a stand. He had these cool twists in his hair. There should be no surprise that the barbers on army posts only knew one style: buzz cut. Nearly every single person we saw greeted Shelby by name.

"How's it going, Sal?" she asked a jolly-looking man as we passed by a pizzeria. "Any news?"

"All's good, Shelby!" He waved happily at her. "Do you and your friend want a free pie?"

"No, thanks," she replied as she kept her fast pace up. Sal simply shook his head and walked back into his restaurant.

"Did you just say no to free pizza?" *Who does that?* And why was he offering it to *her?*

"I have things to do, places to be."

Okay, but still. *Who turns down free pizza?*

I ignored my now rumbling stomach and tried to keep up with Shelby. It didn't matter if the person was old or young, female or male, black or white (or Asian or Latino—and I thought army posts were diverse), everybody seemed happy to see Shelby.

They obviously knew something I didn't.

"So this is a pretty friendly and safe neighborhood, huh?" I asked. I assumed a big city like New York wouldn't be the kind of place where your neighbors were your friends, but maybe I was wrong.

"It depends."

"On what?"

"On who you are," she said with a confident swagger that was usually reserved for professional ballplayers.

I did my best not to laugh at her. I mean, seriously? She wasn't even four feet tall. The baggy jean shorts and purple T-shirt she was wearing made her skinny stature stick out even more. It looked as if her hair hadn't seen a comb in months. She seemed *exactly* like the kind of person people would mess with.

But what did I know? I was the new kid, and everybody in the neighborhood seemed to respect her.

"Ah, just the person I wanted to see!" She jogged over to the corner, where a scruffy white guy with long dreads (I wished the army barbers could've seen this!) was going through the trash. "Seen anything unusual today?"

"Naw." He rubbed his scraggly beard. "You know I'd tell you if I did."

She nodded as she pulled out a banana from her over-sized backpack. "Thanks, Billy." Then she tossed the perfectly good banana into the trash can between them.

"Thanks, Shelby!" Billy removed the banana from the trash and shuffled away.

"He's a freegan," she explained, sensing my bewilderment. "He believes in only eating food that's already been thrown away. Strange, perhaps, but it also means he's quite knowledgeable about what people have in their trash. That's a handy contact."

I had no idea what she was talking about but nodded anyway. I figured it was time for me to get the answers I was really interested in. "How did you know all those details about my mom?"

"What?" She was examining the headlines of a discarded newspaper.

"How did you know my mom served in Afghanistan?"

"Oh, that," she replied, like it was no big deal. Like everybody could read minds. "It's fairly simple. First, your moving boxes had the names of a few army posts written on them, so I knew you were a military family. There was a medical license on the counter. The sole of your mother's right shoe was worn down considerably compared to her left, which means she favors her right side. Based on the boxes, I deduced that an injury sustained during a tour of duty was likely. That meant either Iraq or Afghanistan. Judging by her age and her barely strained gait, I assumed she hasn't been abroad in about two years. Therefore, Afghanistan was my conclusion."

"But you were only in the apartment for a minute!"

"So?" Her attention was now on a few posted flyers.

"That's really . . ." I struggled to come up with the right word. Everything she'd said was true. Every. Last. Detail. "Amazing."

She lit up. "Why, thank you! It's nice to have a contemporary appreciate my talents. *For once.*"

I asked the question I was afraid to know the answer to. "What did you figure out about me?"

She arched her eyebrow. "Do you really want to know?"

Yeah, no. No way did I want to know whatever theory she'd concocted about me. Because there was a very good chance she'd be right. I'd prefer to be left in the dark.

I had to get her off my scent. "But *how* did you do it?"

She exhaled loudly as Sir Arthur examined some weeds growing from the sidewalk. "I observe. Then I assemble all my observations into several different theories and pick the one with the likeliest narrative. It's called deductive reasoning. I don't understand why others don't do it. I realize some people find my observations rude, but I do know when to stay silent. For instance, I didn't bring up your parents' divorce."

I kicked a stray rock onto the road. At this point, I wasn't surprised that she'd figured that out, too.

"When I was talking to the mover, your mom was twisting her ring finger, which no longer sports a ring. Force of habit, I presume. Six months ago?"

"Seven," I answered glumly. Which was also the amount of time since I'd picked up a pen. Until this morning.

"My sincerest regrets." She patted me on the back, which I could tell wasn't a natural gesture for her. My own powers of observation told me that Shelby Holmes was not the touchy-feely type. And that she was disappointed her guess was wrong by a month.

Shelby had already figured out too much, so I tried to not show any emotion on my face as I thought about Dad. He was such a huge part of my life on the army post. Well, of course he was—he was my dad. He worked in the recruiting office and had better hours than Mom, so I would see him more. Then Mom went abroad and Dad was all I had until she returned. Now it was just Mom and me. Mom probably thought that being in a new home and city would make us miss him less. In fact, it made it worse. I felt even more alone.

I didn't want to think about that. It hurt too much. I also didn't want Shelby to do any more of her Jedi mind tricks, so I tried to distract her.

"What about your parents?"

"Married."

"What do they do?"

"They work at Columbia University."

"Figures that your parents are college professors," I replied. Only two Ivy League brainiacs could produce someone like her.

Shelby stopped quickly in her tracks. A high-pitched sound that resembled a laugh escaped her throat. "*My parents? You think my parents are professors? They are about as far from professors as it gets. How did you ever draw that conclusion?*"

Her laughter stung. "Well, you don't have to laugh at me," I snapped. "I was only asking you a question. You said they worked at Columbia. My *sincerest regrets* I couldn't deduce their profession based on your shoelaces."

Shelby studied me for a second, and the scowl that had formed on her face had softened. "I wasn't laughing *at* you.

I was laughing at the idea of my parents as professors. My father is the officer manager in the administration department, while my mother works as an assistant in the financial aid department. We live in the same building, so there's a distinct probability you'll meet them soon, as well as my brother, Michael. He's sixteen. Anything else?"

"Ah," I stammered, not expecting her to be so open with me.

"I'm . . . I'm sorry." Her face scrunched up as if the word *sorry* caused her pain. It probably wasn't a word she used often. "I'm not used to people in my age bracket wanting to get to know me. They usually stay far away from me when they know what I can do."

I was about to apologize to her, but her attention wasn't on me anymore. She was looking at flyers that had been posted on an abandoned storefront. It was like she was searching for something. Or it was possible she was simply bored.

I couldn't imagine being bored in a place like New York City with so many places to go, even though I was too intimidated to go to any of them by myself.

"Where do you go to school?" I asked.

She yanked down an outdated flyer. "I'm pleased to inform you that we'll be attending the same school."

"How did—" I started to ask, but realized she must've seen something in our apartment.

Mom spent months researching schools in New York City before we moved. The Harlem Academy of the Arts, a charter school only a few blocks from our apartment, was first on her list. As she kept telling anybody who asked, it had "an excellent academic as well as arts curriculum." I'd been accepted into the creative writing program.

It figured that Shelby would be in an academically challenging school. I simply hadn't pegged her as someone with an artistic side.

"Violin," she answered before I even had a chance to ask. "I also dabble in acting. It's good practice for going undercover."

Undercover?

She skipped over to a barbershop on the corner where a few guys were sitting outside, fanning themselves in the mid-August heat. Sir Arthur helped himself to the water bowl out front.

"Why, Miss Shelby Holmes!" An older guy with more salt than pepper in his hair reached into his pocket and handed her a butterscotch wrapped in yellow cellophane. "You staying out of trouble, or you trying to find some?"

Shelby unwrapped the candy. "What do *you* think?"

The men erupted into a chorus of laughter.

"Who you got over there?" The man gestured at me to come forward.

"Mr. Washington, this is John Watson. He moved into 221A with his mother, a former army doctor. John, Mr. Washington runs this barbershop and knows *almost* as much as I do about what's happening in our neighborhood."

"Well, well, well . . ." He gave me a once-over. I stuck my chest out a bit, wanting his approval. "Listen here, son, you grow your hair out a bit more, and I'll treat you to a nice new style. Any friend of Shelby's is a friend of mine."

First pizza, then a haircut. Why was everybody offering her free stuff? I mean, the haircut was technically for me, but it was because I was a friend of Shelby's. Well, we weren't really friends, but I wasn't going to argue with him. Free was free.

Shelby waved good-bye as she crossed the street. "You'll like the Academy." She continued our conversation from before without missing a beat. "I'll also be in sixth grade."

I nearly tripped over the curb. "How old are you?"

"I'm nine, but I skipped a couple of grades."

Of course she had. "You don't look nine."

"I'm aware," she said, kneeling down to pet Sir Arthur. "It doesn't bother me. I think it's best to look as young as possible."

"Why?" All I wanted was to grow up and stop being thought of as a little kid.

"Adults always underestimate kids, *especially* girls. It does have its advantages. If you saw me on the street, you'd probably ignore me. Most people do," she said without an ounce of pity. "It allows me to study my marks without worrying about getting caught."

Her *marks*? At this point, I decided to stop asking questions. I didn't think I'd ever understand this girl.

"Plus, I've been practicing jujitsu for a few years, so I'm stronger than I look. Believe me, I'm not somebody people want to mess with."

Oh, I believed her all right. I'd known her for less than twenty-four hours and I already knew not to get on her bad side.

"Now let's focus on you," Shelby said as I tensed up. "We've got to do something about your name."

"What's wrong with my name?"

"Well, there are two other Johns in our class. John Wu goes by John, and John Bryant goes by Bryant. So you'll need a sobriquet. I'm going to refer to you as Watson. It suits you. Trust me, you could be called worse things."

I was sure Shelby Holmes had been called more than a few names. *Know-it-all* was one that sprang to mind.

"Okay," I agreed, knowing it didn't really matter what I wanted to be called. She would've given me whatever name suited her.

As we rounded another corner, Shelby's eyes got big. She looked like a little kid on Christmas morning.

There, parked outside a deli on the opposite side of the street was a cop car with its lights flashing.

Shelby clapped her hands together excitedly. "Watson, I've got work to do."

CHAPTER
3

BEFORE MOM AND I MOVED, DAD SAT ME DOWN FOR A TALK about living in the "real world" (aka not on an army post). One thing he told me was that I shouldn't go looking for trouble, especially where the police were involved.

Apparently, Shelby's dad never had that talk with her, since she handed me Sir Arthur's leash and marched up to the police officers. "Hello, officers. What's going on?"

"Shelby!" An older white guy wearing an apron that matched his white hair emerged from the deli. "Look at what they did to my storefront!"

The metal security gate that was drawn over one side of the deli had A GHRA spray-painted across it in big red letters.

"Tell me everything that happened, Kristos," Shelby insisted.

The deli's name was Kristos, so I deduced he was the owner.

(See, Shelby wasn't the only person who could figure out things without being told!

So there.

John Watson: one. Shelby Holmes: a gazillion.)

Before Kristos could tell his story, a woman with a badge on her belt appeared from inside the deli. She groaned upon seeing Shelby. "Leave this to the police, Holmes. We can handle this without your interference."

"I'm sure you can, Detective Lestrade." Shelby smiled sweetly at her. It was the first time I'd seen her smile, and it looked really unnatural on her.

"It's a basic case of vandalism, end of story."

"Then you shouldn't mind if I take a teensy look around?" she asked the detective, her tone innocent. Shelby then turned toward Kristos. "Would you get me a Fudgsicle? I'm going to need *a lot* of sugar for this."

Kristos obediently ran into the deli.

"Holmes," the detective scolded. "I told you, we've got this."

"Just like you had the guy who robbed Sal's last month?"

Lestrade narrowed her eyes. "That was pure luck, kid."

Ah! The free pizza finally made sense. (Shelby turning down said free pizza was still a mystery.)

"Just a quick glance." Shelby reached into her backpack and took out a measuring tape. She began to measure the graffiti from every angle. She took a few steps back and then paced some more, talking to herself the entire time, until Kristos handed her the Fudgsicle.

Sir Arthur was lying on the ground, his legs stretched out. He knew we were going to be a while.

While Shelby studied the graffiti, I tried to think of what A GHRA could stand for.

This was what I came up with: absolutely nothing.

It was five letters. That wasn't a lot of evidence.

For a regular person.

Shelby approached the detective, who was talking to a fellow officer. "I assume you've been able to deduce that the vandal was Irish, about six foot one, with a rotator cuff injury on their right arm? Most likely a baseball pitcher. I doubt there are a great many people in the area who fit that description."

"Is that true?" the police officer asked Lestrade. "How does she know that?"

"It's quite simple," Shelby began to explain. "Generally, people write at eye level, and this graffiti is fairly high up on the gate, which explains the vandal's height. Also, handwriting tends to slope upward. This gradually slopes downward. That leads me to presume that the person's shoulder has limited range. *A ghrá* is Irish for 'my love.' The apartment building across the street is known as Little Dublin since the majority of residents are Irish students attending Columbia. This appears to be an act of love." Her nose twitched as if she smelled something gross.

"That's incredible," the officer remarked with his mouth slightly agape. His eyes lit up. "You're that girl? I've heard about you!" Lestrade quickly waved him off.

"New guy," Lestrade muttered. "While it's always a pleasure to watch you work"—Lestrade said it in a way that let you know she felt *exactly* the opposite—"there's no need to blow this out of proportion. Vandalism happens every day. We're not going on a wild-goose chase for some guy solely because of your hunches. Seriously, Holmes, what do you expect us to do?"

Shelby stood up tall to the detective, although she was still two feet shorter than her. "How about your job?"

Uh-oh.

I might've been new to the neighborhood, but I was pretty sure getting sassy with a police officer was never a wise move. For anybody. I took a few steps back, wondering if I would draw suspicion if I ran as far away from Shelby as I could. Although I realized that not only did I have no idea where I was, we were definitely farther away than ten blocks. First day on my own and I already broke one of Mom's rules.

"I don't have time for this, Holmes." Lestrade turned toward Kristos. "Call if you discover anything missing," she said before walking away.

The deli owner stood there, looking helpless.

"Don't worry, Kristos." Shelby crossed her arms defiantly. "I'll get someone to clean up this mess until it's as good as new. I have a few people who owe me a favor or two."

The short, stout man patted her on the head, a move that did not make Shelby extremely happy. "You take such good care of me. Do you want some more chocolate?"

"Like you need me to answer that."

"What about your friend?"

Shelby seemed surprised I was still there. "Oh, Watson? He's diabetic, so he should probably have something else, like a piece of fruit or nuts."

"How did—" I stopped myself. Of course Shelby knew I was diabetic. Was there anything she *didn't* know?

I declined Kristos's kind offer, since I was still craving pizza. We began walking home, mostly in silence. Shelby enjoyed her candy bar while I kept trying to figure her out. I went with John Watson's Foolproof Way to Make New Friends: ask questions and let the person talk until you find some sort of common ground. It was something that I'd perfected over the years (and many moves).

"What type of music do you like?" I asked.

"Classical."

"Favorite class?"

"Science."

"Oh, yeah?"

No response.

I continued, "What kind of things do you do with your friends?"

Shelby replied by licking her fingers, which were caked in melted chocolate.

So much for that foolproof plan (since now I felt like a fool). Shelby was a tough code to crack.

I slowed down as we approached our brownstone, wondering if I should invite her to our apartment. We didn't have cable or Internet set up yet, but I could find the box with our DVD player. Maybe we could watch a movie. Or maybe she'd want to go to a park and toss a ball around. Something. Anything.

It wasn't like I thought she and I could be friends, but she was the only person I'd met close to my age. My options were limited. I didn't want to spend the afternoon alone, surrounded by boxes. While I was used to the moving, I didn't think I'd ever get used to being in this huge city, especially without Dad.

Shelby continued her rapid pace and took the stairs leading to the front door, with Sir Arthur trailing behind her. "Good-bye, Watson." She didn't even look at me before the front door slammed shut.

I found myself standing outside our building, unnerved by how quiet our block was in the middle of the afternoon.

Now what was I supposed to do?

CHAPTER 4

"WHAT'D YOU DO TODAY?" MOM ASKED AS SHE WASHED SOME strawberries in the sink.

It was a normal question, but I wasn't sure how to respond. I couldn't make sense of Shelby. At first, she seemed like a really weird girl. Okay, she *still* seemed like a bit of a weirdo, but I couldn't help but be impressed by everything she could do.

"Um, I walked around the neighborhood a bit with Shelby."

Mom paused. "The girl from upstairs?"

"That would be the one." It wasn't like either of us knew anybody else in this place besides Mrs. Hudson.

"That sounds like fun. What did you see?"

I debated how much to tell Mom. She had some sort of lie detector in her brain and she could always, and I mean *always*, tell when I wasn't being truthful. She was also pretty understanding, but to a point.

"We just walked around. I saw this pizza place that looks good. And, um, we may have gone more than ten blocks." I started talking really fast, hoping she would hear me out before she got mad. "But everybody knows Shelby and she's lived in the neighborhood her entire life and I didn't think it was a big deal. Plus, she has this dog and knows jujitsu and at no point did I feel threatened or unsafe." (Well, except for Shelby threatening my self-esteem, but that was an entirely different matter.)

Mom dried off her hands. "Well, I'm sure she does, but I want you to be careful. This is a very different place from anywhere we've lived before."

Oh, how true that was. We were pretty contained on the posts. There was only so much trouble you could find. But I had a feeling that New York City was the kind of place where it could find you. As I thought about Shelby, I wondered if trouble had already met me.

"When you're alone, I only want you going ten blocks," Mom reminded me while she kept opening the kitchen cabinets. This always happened in each new home, trying to remember where we'd put everything. For people who moved a lot, we sure did have a ton of stuff. "Did you unpack the bowls today?"

I looked around at the boxes that still littered the kitchen and living room. "No."

Mom sighed, not the annoyed sigh that Shelby had perfected, but the sigh of someone really tired. "I asked you to unpack more boxes."

"Sorry." I took the scissors off the island and began opening the boxes marked KITCHEN to find our dishes.

Mom placed her hands on my shoulders. "You know, John, we're staying here for good. There's no need to keep anything in boxes anymore. *This* is our home now."

Home. It was something I'd wanted for so long, but I still couldn't picture us here long-term. I still couldn't picture a life without Dad.

"Listen"—she leaned down so we were eye-to-eye, although she didn't have to bend down as much as she used to, since I'd grown a few inches this summer—"I know you're used to being in a new place, but this is different. Do you want to talk about it?"

I shook my head. Mom always wanted to have "open conversations" about how I was feeling about the divorce and being so far away from Dad, who moved back to Kentucky.

She gave me a tight smile and pulled me in for a hug. "I understand how difficult this has been on you and know you'll adjust to life here. You'll be in school in three weeks and won't have any trouble making friends—you never have."

Three more weeks of being alone in this city? I mean, I know I wasn't *alone* alone, but Mom had work. I had only boxes to keep me company.

"Tomorrow afternoon I want you to come up to the medical center to meet with your new diabetes doctor. I made an appointment with her at four, and then afterward I'll show you around my new workplace. I'll leave you some money on the counter for a taxi. I don't want you taking the subway or bus by yourself just yet. We both need to get used to the city first. Sound good?"

I said the only thing I could: "Yep."

Because I really didn't have any other choice. Or anything else to do.

CHAPTER
5

I SPENT THE NEXT MORNING UNPACKING MORE BOXES UNTIL boredom got the best of me. After an early lunch, I found myself sitting on our outside stoop again. While I had my journal in my hand, I realized that I was waiting. I almost didn't want to admit it to myself, but it was very clear what I was waiting for. Oh, who was I kidding? I was waiting for a *who*.

After almost an hour, the front door opened and I tried not to seem too desperate. I stood up as she passed me. "Hey, Shelby!"

She turned around with a scowl on her face. "Do I have to start walking you now, too?"

Sir Arthur looked up from the tree that had his attention for a moment before going back to sniffing. *He* didn't really seem to mind . . .

"I just thought, you know, like I could, um, walk around with you, and, um . . ." I stammered. I never had this tough

of a time connecting with someone before, but generally, when I'm talking to somebody, they aren't looking at me with contempt.

This was a bad idea.

Shelby turned on her heel. "Well, come on, then."

Not the most welcoming gesture, but I followed her. I wasn't exactly sure what my plan was, but hanging out with Shelby was way better than being alone in the apartment.

"So you're a detective?" I asked to break the silence. Plus, how cool was that? A detective!

"Yes," she replied as she kept up her speedy pace.

"Um, but, like, how?"

"By solving cases."

"So did you just always know how to—"

Shelby cut me off. "Watson, what is it that you want?"

What did I *want?* I didn't understand why she was so angry all of a sudden. "I want to get to know you better, that's all. I think all the stuff you do is really cool. I'm sorry if I seem nosy, but whenever I got to a new post, I liked to get to know the friends I met."

"Oh," she said with a softer voice. "I'm not used to people asking me things without wanting anything."

"It's okay." We walked in silence for a few minutes. I didn't want to push her, but it was clear she didn't want to talk.

"It's something that I've always been good at," Shelby

finally said. "Ever since I was little, I could remember facts and have been curious about how things work. My brother's the same way. Well, in the fact that he's intelligent, not something that I would ever admit to him, but he's also extremely lazy."

"So you have a photographic memory?" I've heard about people who can remember everything they read or see.

"You're referring to eidetic memory, and no. I don't merely regurgitate random facts back. I observe. I analyze. *That* takes talent. It was a hobby, but then two years ago there was a rash of thefts at the school library. I studied the evidence and was able to pin down the culprit using simple powers of observation."

"Wait." I did the math. "You solved your first crime at *seven?*"

Shelby looked upset. "Sadly, yes. I wish I had started sooner so I could have more experience under my belt, but luckily there's enough action in the neighborhood to keep me busy."

"So people, like, call you or—"

"When you're as good as I am, you get a reputation. A *good* reputation. People know each other in this neighborhood. They talk. They know what I can do. Some people like it; others don't."

We turned the corner back onto Baker Street. It was a much shorter walk than yesterday. I couldn't help but wonder if I had anything to do with that.

As we approached our building, I saw somebody standing outside. It was a girl with big brown eyes and curly black hair. "Shelby! Something awful has happened!"

"Really?" Shelby responded to bad news with an enthusiasm that was a little unsettling. "What's going on?"

"Daisy has gone missing! I can't find her anywhere, and the big show's in three days!"

"You've come to the right person, Tamra." Shelby's lips curled into what appeared to be an actual, genuine smile. "This sounds like a case for Shelby Holmes. I'll be right back." Shelby bounded up the stairs with Sir Arthur while I was left alone with the girl.

"Hi, I'm John."

The girl wiped away a stray tear on her cheek. "I'm Tamra."

"I'm sorry about your . . ." I realized that I had no idea who Daisy was.

After a beat of awkward silence, Tamra finally answered, "Daisy's my dog."

"Oh, that's awful. Are you friends with Shelby?"

She shook her head. "Not really. We go to school together."

"I'm going to the Academy, too!" I said with a little too much exuberance to someone who just lost her dog, but I was excited to meet another classmate. "I'm in the creative writing program. What about you?"

"Dance." She gave me a tiny smile. "So you're new to town?"

Finally! Someone who knows how to have a normal conversation. Someone who can't guess everything about me.

"Yeah, I just moved here. Into this building." I pointed at the four-story brownstone that Shelby was now exiting.

"Let's go!" Shelby called out as Tamra walked over to a slick black car that was parked across the street.

I didn't know what to do. Shelby was definitely going to do that Shelby thing she does, and I didn't want to miss it. So for the second day in a row, I found myself calling out to her. "Wait!"

Both girls turned around and looked at me expectantly.

"Can I come along?" I asked, feeling foolish and a little guilty knowing that Mom would definitely not approve. I was basically getting in a car with strangers. And who knew what we were going to get up to?

Tamra looked at Shelby. "Does he work with you?"

Shelby scoffed. "I work alone."

"Well, maybe I can help? I did grow up on army posts and have a lot of experience with the military." Okay, that was stretching it, but maybe there was something I could do to help? Crazier things have happened. (See: everything Shelby Holmes had done in the last forty-eight hours.)

Shelby rolled her eyes at my puffed-up statement. I should've known better than to try that in front of her.

I was about to head inside the house when Tamra shrugged her shoulders. "It's fine with me."

I ran so quickly across the street Shelby didn't have a chance to object. Before I knew it, I was in the car with Shelby and Tamra on our way to solve a crime.

⌐•CHAPTER•⌐
6

SHELBY HOLMES DOESN'T WASTE TIME.

"Tell me everything that's happened," Shelby ordered Tamra. "And don't leave a single detail out."

Tamra wrung her light brown hands in her lap as she started to fill us in. "There's not much to say. I woke up this morning and Daisy was just . . . gone. She sleeps in bed with me, but at some point in the night she'll go downstairs.

So when I woke up and she wasn't there, I didn't think anything of it. But when I went downstairs, she didn't come to greet me. I called her, but she didn't come, and she *always* comes. Then we all looked around the apartment and couldn't find her. At first, I thought that maybe she was locked in a closet, but we looked in all the closets. We looked everywhere. Dad called security and the doormen hadn't seen her since I walked her last night before bed. It's like she vanished."

While I should have been paying attention to the details of the case, I kept getting caught up in the fact that Tamra lived in a building with an elevator, doormen, *and* security. Plus, I didn't need Shelby to tell me that this car and personal driver belonged to her family.

"I can't believe it." Tamra's voice wavered. "The show's in three days. Everybody knows that Daisy's the favorite, but I can't believe someone would take her away from me."

Shelby did need to fill me in that the show Tamra kept talking about was the Manhattan Kennel Club's annual dog show. Daisy came in second last year in the toy breed category.

Toy breed? I nodded like I understood any of that.

"Does Daisy have any enemies?" Shelby asked. I had to stop myself from laughing. How could a dog have enemies?

"Not at all. She's the sweetest dog in the whole world. Although . . ."

Shelby's posture straightened. "Although what?"

"Maybe it's nothing." Tamra bit her lip. "In the last six months, Daisy's taken titles away from Mr. Wiggles, who always used to win. But I don't think Mr. Wiggles's owner even knows where we live, let alone be able to break into our apartment."

"Never underestimate an underdog," Shelby said with a confident nod.

A laugh escaped my throat, and I started coughing to cover it up.

Underdog? Mr. Wiggles? Really? What had I gotten myself into?

The car turned as we headed toward a park that seemed to stretch for miles and miles. I didn't know the city that well yet, but I knew it had to be Central Park. The driver made another turn and pulled up alongside a tall stone building with two towers.

"We're here," Tamra said as she exited the car.

A doorman greeted her as he opened the intricate glass doors that led us into a lobby with marble floors, wood paneling, and mural walls. I felt like we were on the set of some movie about superrich people back in the 1940s. But people actually lived like this. For real.

My grandma once came to Kentucky to visit us. We took a day trip to Nashville since it was the closest big city. Grandma took Mom and me to a fancy hotel for tea. At the time, I couldn't imagine staying even a night at such a nice place, let alone living every single day in such a ridiculously fancy building.

John, you're not in Kentucky anymore.

"Any word, Javier?" Tamra asked the man at the security desk, who was wearing the same gray-and-red uniform as the doorman.

He shook his head solemnly. "Nothing, but don't you worry, Miss Lacy. We'll find your Daisy."

Another man tipped his cap as he hit the elevator button for Tamra.

Once we got inside, Shelby started talking in a whisper. "Tamra, I need you to inform your family and whoever else we meet that we are familiar acquaintances. I can't have people know I'm here to investigate. This way, they'll be more natural around me and I can study them freely."

"But nobody in my family would do this—they all love Daisy," Tamra protested.

The elevator came to a stop on the twenty-fourth floor. Once we were inside the apartment, I stopped in my tracks. Although the building appeared to be old, Tamra's apartment was the exact opposite. It was like I stepped into some futuristic home. Everything was made of glass, white marble, shiny silver, or leather. Every item looked new, expensive, and extremely breakable. I was afraid to walk around for fear that I'd accidentally smash one of the large glass vases overflowing with flowers that seemed to be on every surface.

I'd never seen anything like it.

(I need to start getting out more.)

"You're home!" a voice cried out. A woman who had the same big brown eyes as Tamra hugged her and said, "I know you're upset, but don't go running off like that, okay? We can't have any more members of the family go missing."

"I'm sorry, Mom." Tamra hugged her back. "I went to find some friends."

"Hi, Mrs. Lacy!" Shelby's voice was a lot louder than normal (which was saying a lot). "Yes, we are *friends*. Great *friends!* Allow me to introduce myself, since I have not yet had the good fortune to make your acquaintance. I'm Shelby Holmes. I attend school with Tamra!" She then laughed really hard as if someone had told a joke.

Was this Shelby being calm undercover? If so, we were in trouble.

"Ah, I'm John Watson," I said to distract everybody from Shelby's jittery behavior, and shook Mrs. Lacy's hand like *a normal person would do.* "Nice to meet you, ma'am. You have a nice home."

"Thank you, John." Mrs. Lacy looked around the apartment nonchalantly.

"Why, yes, it is rather lovely." Shelby put her arm around Tamra, who in turn placed her head in her hand, probably wondering what she was thinking, asking Shelby over. "Well done!"

Mrs. Lacy tilted her head at Shelby, perhaps curious as to why Tamra would've chosen this tense time to bring home a new friend, especially one acting so uncomfortably. "It's nice to meet you both. Thank you for being here for Tamra. We're all at a loss about what could've possibly happened to our Daisy." Mrs. Lacy looked like a model (and more like Tamra's older sister than her mom). Every hair was in place, and she had on about fourteen different pieces of jewelry and sky-high heels (how can girls walk in those things?). I felt out of place in a ratty T-shirt and shorts.

"Has Dad called the cops yet?" Tamra asked, getting us back to the pressing matter of the missing dog.

"Not yet, sweetheart." She wrapped her arms around her daughter.

"Ugh, don't call the cops," Shelby groaned. "I mean, what are the cops going to do? Am I right?" She then snorted so loudly I wanted to crawl into a hole for her.

Mrs. Lacy nodded at Shelby slowly. "Tamra, can I speak with you in private?"

Mrs. Lacy and Tamra went into a room that was off the large living room where we were standing (my guess was that they were going to call the mental ward to haul Shelby away). Shelby sat down on a leather couch while I remained standing, as I was too afraid I'd stain something.

"Are you okay?" I asked.

"Of course, Watson, old chum!"

Old chum? Who talks like that?

"You seem a little nervous," I admitted. While I really didn't know her well, nervous didn't seem like her style. Overly confident maybe, but not nervous.

"I do?" Shelby slouched down on the couch. "I'm usually much better undercover, but I've never had to be someone's friend before."

"Just be like how you are with your real friends."

"Right," she responded quietly.

Of course. The nervous laughter. The awkward body movements. Shelby had difficulty pretending to be a fake friend because she didn't have a lot of real friends. Maybe none at all.

Sure, everybody in the neighborhood was excited to see her, but they were all adults. Shelby had mentioned how her "contemporaries" didn't appreciate her talents. Maybe she didn't have any friends her own age?

Was deductive reasoning contagious? Because I so had this thing down.

"You know," I proceeded cautiously, "I have lots of experience making new friends—one of the talents you get moving around so much. Maybe I can help you?"

Shelby tilted her chin up. "I don't need any help. I'm fine on my own, thank you very much."

"Listen, Shelby—" I began, but there was a scream accompanied by a loud clattering noise that came from down the hallway.

Followed by the sound of a barking dog.

CHAPTER
7

I WAS ON SHELBY'S HEELS AS SHE RACED TOWARD THE noise.

Upon entering the largest kitchen I'd ever seen, a girl a little older than Tamra was trying to calm down a tiny ball of black fur that was barking at an older white woman wearing an apron.

"Get that dog out of here!" the woman cried, her cheeks flushed. "How many times do I have to say it: no animals in the kitchen!"

"Zareen!" A man with a suit on entered the kitchen and snapped his fingers. "Get her out, right now. You know better!"

Zareen picked up the dog, who turned her incessant barking at me before being whisked away.

"You found her!" I started saying before I could help myself. "Where was she?"

"That's not Daisy," Shelby informed me. "Daisy is a Cavalier King Charles spaniel. That Pomeranian is Zareen's dog, Roxy."

"And Zareen is—"

"Tamra's older sister."

"Are you okay, Eugenia?" the man asked the woman, who was shaking considerably from the incident.

"Yes, Mr. Lacy." Her voice had some sort of accent. Australian? Scottish? Irish? I had a hard time telling the difference. The woman wiped her hands on her apron and went back to cutting up some vegetables. "I didn't mean to scream so loudly. I was simply taken by surprise."

"I'll go talk to her," Mr. Lacy said with a sigh. "Again."

"So you're from Essex?" Shelby asked the woman.

The woman appeared startled that there were other people in the kitchen. "Oh, why, yes. My, you certainly have an ear for accents. Tell me, my dears, who might you be?"

"They're my friends," Tamra replied upon entering the kitchen with her mother right behind her.

"Would your friends like a snack?"

I looked at Shelby, hoping she wasn't going to say no to another offer for free food. Pizza was one thing, but I was fairly certain that this woman was a professional chef, and there was no way I wanted to turn down whatever she made in this ginormous kitchen.

Shelby smiled widely at her. "I'd be delighted to partake in the walnut-fudge brownies you made this morning, please." She sat herself down at the booth that was in the corner of the kitchen.

The woman looked around. "How did you know I made a batch this morning?"

I found myself copying Mrs. Hudson from the first time I met Shelby. "It's just this thing she does."

I had a feeling I'd be repeating that phrase a lot if I continued hanging out with Shelby.

"However," Shelby continued, "Watson should probably have something else, like an apple, but with some peanut butter to help stabilize his blood sugar."

Before I could protest, Shelby turned to me. "In all the excitement, I hadn't noticed how much time had passed. You must be hungry."

I was. I had breakfast with my mom and made a sandwich for lunch, and then I went out on the stoop. Usually I would've had a snack an hour or so ago.

We sat down as Miss Eugenia, who was in fact the Lacys' personal chef, served Tamra and Shelby brownies with milk, while I tried not to be too jealous as I took a bite of my Granny Smith apple (which might've been the best-tasting apple I'd ever had—did rich people get their apples from a different place than us common folk?).

Once the grumbling in our stomachs subsided, we took stock of what we knew so far, which wasn't very much.

"Has Daisy ever come into the kitchen?" Shelby took a bite of another brownie.

(Her third, not like I was counting.

Okay, I was.)

"Never," Tamra said with a fierce shake of her head. "Even if the door's wide open, Daisy wouldn't come in here. She knows the rules."

"And what about Roxy?"

Tamra glanced at the door and then lowered her voice. "Roxy's always been a handful. Zareen wanted her to compete in dog shows also, but she always barks at strangers."

"But Miss Eugenia isn't a stranger. She's been working for your family since before you were born."

Tamra didn't bother asking Shelby how she knew that fact about Miss Eugenia, although I looked around, trying to find the clue that made her take that leap. I was too busy being in awe of the shiny marble floor. It was like being in a museum.

Tamra continued, "Well, Roxy doesn't bark at immediate family, although she sometimes barks at my dad. It drives him crazy. He wanted to get rid of Roxy since she's so loud, and a few neighbors have even complained. But anytime he brings it up, Zareen locks herself in her room and she won't come out until he promises her she can keep Roxy."

"Interesting." Shelby nodded slowly. "And where was Roxy when Daisy disappeared?"

"Roxy sleeps in the hallway downstairs at the foot of the stairs. She only moves to her bed in the dogs' room if Daisy is with her. Roxy isn't allowed to sleep in Zareen's room anymore, because she kept chewing on the furniture. We close all the other doors, except for the dogs' room, so she won't cause too much trouble during the night."

"And where was she when you realized that Daisy had gone missing?"

"Roxy was in the hallway chewing on one of Daisy's toys."

"And was it a toy that Daisy would've gone to bed with?"

"Yes." Tamra slapped her hand against her forehead. "I'm just realizing this now. Daisy always brings Caruso to bed—that's the name of her stuffed Chihuahua—as well as a stuffed bone, which also wasn't in my bed this morning. She must've taken them with her when she went to keep Roxy company in the middle of the night. She likes to do that sometimes. I think Daisy feels bad for Roxy."

"But how did she get out of your room if the door was shut so Roxy wouldn't get in?" I blurted out, proud that I could contribute something to this investigation.

"Because the bedrooms are on the second floor," Shelby replied before turning back to Tamra. "I assume Roxy is either too small to get up the stairs by herself or is afraid of the stairs?"

"Actually, it's both. She'll sometimes just bark at the stairs." Tamra shook her head.

"But you said that she sleeps near the stairs? Why would she do that if she was scared of them?" Shelby asked.

"She used to sit there and whine, hoping one of us would take her up to the second floor. I think she does it because it requires whoever goes downstairs to have to pet her or make some fuss over her since she's in the way."

"Are there any exits on the second floor?" Shelby asked.

"None."

"And would it be possible for somebody to leave the apartment without passing Roxy?"

"No. We only have the one staircase, which is near the one door."

"Interesting. Can you give us a tour?"

I always hated it whenever Mom insisted that we take the dreaded house tour when we visited friends and family, like I really cared about a powder room. But I was looking forward to this one. I already couldn't wait to tell Mom all about it. I didn't understand how we could've called this palace and the small two-bedroom place where we moved into the same thing. Was there such a thing as a mega-apartment?

"Of course," Tamra replied, but then her name was called from the hallway. "I'll be right back."

Shelby shut her eyes for a few minutes while I tried to put everything together. Who would've wanted Daisy gone?

"Maybe the cook did it?" I offered.

"No," she replied with closed eyes.

"You're only saying that because she gave you brownies."

She finally opened her eyes. It was clear that I had somehow insulted her. "I can't be bribed."

"Okay, okay, but she doesn't like dogs," I reasoned. "She would've had access."

"It wasn't the cook."

"How do you know?"

"Isn't it obvious?"

Uh, no. It wasn't obvious or I wouldn't have suggested it.

"I'm surprised with your vast *experience with the military* that you would draw such a conclusion," Shelby teased. (Honestly, I was impressed she held out this long before she took a dig at my exaggerated experience.) "Besides, there's something way more pressing, Watson. I've just had a huge clue delivered right to me."

"What clue?"

"Whoever took Daisy would've had to pass by or be near Roxy, but Roxy didn't make any noise last night or this morning. Isn't that curious?"

"Why?"

"Because the dog barks at almost everybody."

"So?"

"*So* that would mean that whoever took Daisy was someone who Roxy knew. It had to have been a close family member or a friend. Or else Roxy would've barked so much when the person went to leave that it would've woken the whole apartment, if not the building."

Oh.

Shelby took another brownie off the plate (and *I'm* the one with the insulin problem?). "It looks like I can put everybody in the family on my list of suspects."

"Isn't it innocent until proven guilty?" I asked.

"Not for me. It's guilty until proven otherwise."

CHAPTER 8

A CRIME HAD DEFINITELY BEEN COMMITTED IN TAMRA'S room.

There was pink *everywhere*. If a surface wasn't bubblegum pink, it was covered in something frilly. The entire top of Tamra's pink dresser was crowded with first-place trophies in dance and dog competitions. Above her bed was a large painting of a black-and-white dog with brown around the eyes.

I felt like I was getting hives simply from being in here.

"Where does Daisy usually sleep?" Shelby asked.

When Tamra patted the place on the bed next to where she had sat down, Shelby hopped on the bed on all fours like a dog. She then put her face so low there was hardly any room between her nose and the pink lace comforter. After a few minutes of actually sniffing around, she jumped down to the ground and continued her, *ah*, research?

Tamra looked up at me with a quizzical expression, and all I could do was shrug. Like *I* had any clue what Shelby was up to.

"So this was how she would've left?" Shelby asked from the floor as she sniffed the doorway.

"Yeah." Tamra had a horrified look on her face, probably wondering what *she* had gotten herself into.

We followed our pseudo four-legged companion out into the hallway.

"What's in those rooms?" Shelby gestured at the two rooms across the hall.

"Those are Zareen's and Zane's rooms," Tamra replied as she opened one of the doors. "They're twins."

Shelby stood up and scanned Zareen's room, which was painted a sunny yellow. It had far less clutter and trophies than Tamra's. The trophies she did have were for third and fourth place.

It didn't take a genius like Shelby Holmes to wonder if Zareen might have had a motive to take Daisy. Her younger sister got all the trophies and had the better-behaved dog who most likely would've won Saturday's competition. Plus, Roxy wouldn't bark at her.

We moved on to the next room. Suddenly, I felt hopeful. Zane wasn't only a guy; he was my kind of guy: posters of the New York Yankees and the Knicks lined his dark blue walls. On his bookshelves were pictures with other guys at an amusement park and playing ball.

I needed to meet this guy, ASAP.

Unfortunately, Shelby wasn't too interested in his room and we moved back into the hallway. She traced her finger along a bureau that lined the wall. She looked at her finger and sighed. "This house is so clean there's hardly any dust."

"You say that like it's a bad thing," I remarked.

Shelby lowered her face so it was level with the top of the bureau. "Dust can be a detective's best friend—you can see what *wasn't* left behind."

"So do you have any leads?" Tamra asked, her patience deteriorating.

"A few."

Shelby dropped back down to the floor and started pacing back and forth like a dog.

"Ah, hello?" a voice called out from the stairs. I turned around and saw Zane. He had a large duffel bag slung around his chest and a basketball in his hand. "Any word on Daisy?"

"None." Tamra's eyes began to well with tears.

"Don't worry, sis, we'll find—" Zane stopped, his head tilted toward Shelby, who was now sniffing the corner of the bureau.

I needed to do damage control as this was my chance to make friends with someone who wasn't trying to impersonate a dog. "Hey, man, I'm John."

"Zane." He jerked his chin at me, and it was eerie how much he looked like Zareen—same profile and almond-shaped eyes, except instead of a mass of curls on his head, he had short hair with a slight wave. *That's* the style I'm going to ask Mr. Washington for when my hair grows out from my buzz cut. "What's up, John? You live in the building?"

"Naw." I was flattered he thought I could've ever belonged in a place like that. "Just a friend of your sister's."

"You with her?" He frowned at Shelby, whose backside was sticking up in the air, which I could only assume was her attempt to observe every fiber in the carpet.

"We live in the same building," I explained. "I only met her two days ago. I'm new here, just moved from Maryland."

"Cool, you play ball?" Zane threw his basketball at me, which I caught, thankfully. There were picture frames covering the bureau in the hallway, and the last thing I wanted to do was break anything.

"Yeah, man," I replied nonchalantly, although all I wanted was for him to invite me along. I didn't want to have to wait three more weeks for school to make friends.

Before I could've made any plans with Zane, Tamra

started sobbing. She was looking at a photo she'd picked up from the bureau. "I'm sick thinking that Daisy is out there somewhere and that someone could be hurting her."

Shelby stood back up and brushed her hands on her shorts. "The person who took Daisy has no intention of hurting her. It was someone she knows."

"What?" Tamra put the photo down so hard she knocked a few other frames over. "Why would you say that?"

"Because Roxy didn't bark when Daisy was taken."

Tamra's mouth was practically on the floor. "You're right! I didn't think about that."

"Of course *you* didn't," Shelby stated bluntly.

It seemed like such a simple piece of evidence: Roxy, the dog that barks incessantly, didn't bark when Daisy was taken from downstairs. Yet everybody overlooked it. Except Shelby.

Tamra's hands were trembling as she put the picture frames back in place. "Wait a second." She began picking up the different pictures and examining them. "One of the pictures is missing."

"Really?" Shelby asked excitedly.

"Are you sure?" Zane asked as he came over to inspect the photos. "Mom probably rotated them or something. It's not like she can leave a room alone for too long without redecorating it."

"No, it was here yesterday. I remember showing Shayla the photo of us in London when she was over. It was right here." Tamra pointed to the left corner.

"What kind of frame was it?" Shelby inquired. "Crystal? Antique?"

"None of these frames are expensive," Zane stated. "We don't have a lot of antiques on this floor."

"Ah, because Zareen sleepwalks," Shelby stated to the shock of the group. "It was pretty evident from the extra locks on her windows, heavy curtains, bell at her bedroom door, and prescription on her dresser. You should've been concerned if I hadn't noticed that. After all, I'm the one who's going to find your dog."

So much for our cover.

Zane scratched his head. "Ah, *that's* what you're doing here? Mom said Tamra had friends over, not some *detectives.*" He said *detectives* with a sneer. I remembered what Shelby said earlier about being underestimated. I would've also doubted her had I not witnessed her in action.

Tamra crossed her arms. "Listen, Zane, Shelby's the smartest person in the entire school. She was the one who figured out who had stolen the money from the dance department's fund-raiser. The principal didn't even bother with the police, she's *that* good. Nobody knows that Zareen sleepwalks, but she figured that out simply by being in her room for a couple minutes."

I looked over at Shelby, who smirked back at Zane, clearly annoyed that she'd have to prove herself to anybody.

Zane laughed. "Yeah, okay. Call me crazy, but that doesn't really instill a ton of faith in me. Anybody can read a prescription bottle. Congratulations."

Shelby ignored Zane's dig. "Do we know if she had an episode last night?"

"No." Zane put his hands in his pockets. "Zareen hardly sleepwalks anymore."

"I KNEW IT!" Zareen's voice boomed as she stomped up the stairs, her curls bouncing with every step. "I KNEW you were going to find a way to blame me. I didn't do it! But, of course, perfect Tamra couldn't be held accountable for losing her own dog."

"It's not my fault you're jealous of me," Tamra spit back at her older sister.

"Don't listen to her, Zareen." Zane placed his arm around his twin.

"Oh, what a surprise. Zane's taking Zareen's side," Tamra replied sarcastically.

"Tamra," Zane scolded his sister, "don't pick on Zareen. We're all doing everything we can to find Daisy. And, Zareen, nobody thinks you did it."

Tamra stepped forward so she was only inches away from Zareen. "That's not true. *I* think you did it."

With those words, an eruption of accusations overcame the two sisters as they each tried to blame the other for Daisy's disappearance.

"Why would I want my dog to disappear?" Tamra exclaimed as Zane stepped in between his sisters.

"Because all you want is attention!" Zareen tugged on her brother's arm. "You have to admit that Tamra could've totally taken Daisy last night and given her to a friend so she can have Mom and Dad fuss over her even more. As if that were humanly possible."

Shelby leaned toward me and said in a low voice, "Well, Watson, we've arrived at the finger-pointing stage of the investigation where everybody thinks they're a detective."

"Guys!" I tried to get the shouting to stop. Not only was this really uncomfortable, but I also hated watching a family fight. Believe me, I've seen my share of family fighting, and no good could ever come from it. "Can we all just calm down? Please?"

Nothing. It was like I was talking to the walls.

"Let the professional handle this." Shelby rolled her eyes as she approached the siblings in an attempt to restore order. "Would it be possible to display some decorum during these proceedings?"

Shockingly, that did nothing. Mostly because there wasn't a dictionary handy to decipher whatever Shelby was trying to say.

The girls did finally quiet, only because Mrs. Lacy began shouting as she climbed the stairs. "I will not tolerate this behavior in our house! We're all upset Daisy's missing, but that doesn't mean you can blame each other."

"You wouldn't be this upset if Roxy were missing." Zareen glared at her mother.

"Mommy," Tamra cooed sweetly, "did you take the photo of us in London?"

"No." Mrs. Lacy came over to the bureau and searched through the photos. She turned to Zareen. "Did you knock it over in your sleep?"

"WHY DOES EVERYBODY BLAME ME FOR EVERYTHING!" Zareen ran into her room and slammed the door shut.

Once again, the hallway became a battlefield of yelling and accusations, with the added tension of Mrs. Lacy banging on Zareen's door.

It was pure chaos.

Here I always thought having money would make life easier. But apparently money couldn't cure crazy.

Shelby hung her head. "This case is suffering from too many cooks in the kitchen."

"The cook!" I stated again, not being able to shake my suspicion of the antidog chef.

Shelby moaned. "As I explained in the kitchen, it wasn't the chef."

"I'm just saying—"

She cut me off. "What did you notice when we entered the kitchen?"

"What?" It was difficult to concentrate with all the noise the Lacys were making.

Shelby was as focused as ever. "When we entered the kitchen, please tell me everything that you had observed."

My mind went back to our rushing into the kitchen. "Besides the huge kitchen that looked like it belonged on the cover of some cooking magazine? I saw the little dog barking and Zareen trying to control her. Mr. Lacy was yelling at her."

"And that's it?"

"Yeah." What else was there to see?

"This was what I had observed: upon entering the kitchen, I took a sweep of the room. Miss Eugenia was pressed up against the counter with a tissue in her hand. Once Zareen picked up Roxy, Miss Eugenia went into a drawer and pulled out an inhaler, which she quickly used, and then blew her nose. She is extremely allergic to dogs, which is why they aren't allowed in the kitchen. I also noticed that there was a bag of walnuts on the counter and a dish that was drying that could be used to make brownies. I had once observed Tamra eating a delicious walnut-fudge brownie a couple years ago, so that's how I knew what Miss Eugenia baked this morning."

"Wait." I stopped her. "You remember a brownie that someone who isn't even your friend was eating a couple years ago?"

"I never forget a good dessert." Shelby looked wistful as the memory of the brownie no doubt entered her mind. "But I digress. The reason Miss Eugenia couldn't have taken

Daisy is twofold: one, Roxy certainly would've barked at her, as we witnessed earlier, and two, she wouldn't have gotten more than ten feet without having an allergic reaction."

"Oh." Maybe being a detective wasn't as easy as I thought.

Well, at least we now had one less suspect to worry about.

Shelby stepped forward. I could barely hear her over the arguing Lacys—who were only getting louder. "There's a difference between seeing and observing, Watson. You must learn not simply to see, but observe the whole scene that is placed before you. Usually, the answer is right in front of you, *if* you know how to look."

I was so distracted by a little dog that was making a ton of noise I didn't take in anything else. I vowed that I was going to be more observant.

My focus went back to the Lacys as Zareen finally opened her door, but only to continue her heated argument with her mother.

I couldn't believe some of the things Zareen was saying to her mother. If I even raised—

My heart stopped. *My mother.* Who I was supposed to meet this afternoon.

"What time is it?" My voice was near a shrill.

Shelby casually looked at her watch. "Three twenty-two."

"I have to be at the Columbia University Medical Center

at four to meet my mom. She's going to kill me if I'm late."

Shelby didn't look concerned. "Well, you should probably move along, then."

Move along? I had no idea where I was or how to get anywhere. Mom gave me money for a taxi, but that was from our apartment. I didn't know if I had enough money or enough time. "Will a taxi get me there in time?"

Shelby snorted. "In New York City traffic? Good luck."

My panic wasn't being helped by the Lacys constantly bickering.

"Take the one."

"What?"

Shelby threw her head back in exasperation. "Take the one train uptown to 168th Street. You can get it at 86th Street. The ride should be around twenty minutes—you'll make it in time, but you have to leave now."

I remained frozen.

"GAH!" Shelby cried out, which finally quieted everybody down. "Fine, I'll take you. The Lacys are no good to me in this condition anyway." She turned toward the family. "I'll be back first thing tomorrow to look around the apartment and the building. Try not to move anything until then. I'd also appreciate it if you could all calm down and remember everything that has happened since Daisy went on her walk last night. Do we think everybody can handle all that?"

Mrs. Lacy's eyes were wide. "What? What's going on?"

Zane laughed. "She's apparently some detective from school."

Shelby ignored Zane and turned her attention toward Tamra. "I think you need to fill everybody in. We have no time for games and hissy fits."

Tamra nodded while Zareen and Mrs. Lacy looked absolutely flummoxed.

"Come along, Watson," Shelby said over her shoulder.

I obediently followed. I felt foolish that I needed her to escort me, but above all, I felt grateful.

CHAPTER 9

SHELBY LED ME TO THE SUBWAY (MUMBLING UNDER HER breath the entire time about "professionalism") and took me on my very first New York City subway ride as we headed to Mom's work.

I tried not to stare at everybody who entered the subway or grasp the pole too tightly when the train swayed as it made its way uptown. I'd seen the New York City subway countless of times on different TV shows or movies. There I was, riding it like a real New Yorker. Well, a New Yorker who nearly fell over when the subway paused abruptly and I hadn't properly braced myself.

I leaned over to study the many multicolored lines that made up the subway map, remembering the list Mom and I had made of all the places we wanted to see once we settled in: the Statue of Liberty, Coney Island, Yankee Stadium, Madison Square Garden, Little Italy—pretty much all of it! I couldn't wait to really explore. This was my city now.

"What's your favorite place in the city?" I asked Shelby.

"The library."

A library? I mean, I love books and all, but New York City has skyscrapers and museums and celebrities. Must be some library.

"What museums do you go to?"

"All of them."

"Uh, what . . ." I trailed off because I could tell that Shelby's curt replies, while something I was getting used to, were probably due to the fact that I dragged her away from her case. I felt guilty, I really did.

Shelby closed her eyes and began talking to herself. When she finally opened them and looked at me, she appeared disappointed I was still there.

Since she wasn't interested in talking to me about New York City, I figured there was one thing she might be interested in: her case.

"Do you have any idea what happened to Daisy?" I asked.

She shrugged. "Currently there are numerous possibilities. I need to case the residence properly and personally speak to the guards. Doing it a day later generally places me at a disadvantage, as it's imperative to have everybody's memories fresh. However, we have two full days left before the dog show, plenty of time for the thief to make a mistake."

"Do you think the missing picture frame has anything to do with who took Daisy?"

"Perhaps. I don't ignore anything. Sometimes the smallest clue can lead to the biggest discovery."

I nodded. "I'm really sorry again for making you leave. It's really cool of you to help me out."

"I'm used to helping people. Generally, it's something of a more prominent nature, not being a personal tour guide."

I masked my scowl because she was right. I did need her help, but then a thought hit me. "So you go to school with Tamra, but you aren't friends. Doesn't it bother you that she only came to you because she wanted something?"

She shrugged. "It's what I do." She looked away and pretended to read the advertisements on the train, but it was obvious it bothered her. How could it not?

I mean, not like Shelby was the easiest person to get to know or become friends with.

Still, it must've been hard to have people only want to hang out with you if you could do something for them. But wasn't that what I was doing now?

"Hey." I tried to think of something I could do to show her how much I appreciated her help, but I could only think of one thing she truly enjoyed (besides making people feel foolish). "Maybe tomorrow I could buy you, like, I don't know, a huge vat of sugar or something? Is there a bakery or an ice cream place near our building? It would be on me."

"You don't have to do that."

"I know, but I *want* to." Plus, maybe she'll be nicer when she's hopped up on sugar (not like she didn't inhale four brownies earlier).

She finally looked at me. I was expecting gratitude or a crack in her hard exterior, but she was annoyed. "Please don't, Watson."

"Don't what?"

"Pretend we're friends, because the second you meet somebody from our school, you'll act like you don't know me."

Was this because she could tell I wanted to hang with Zane? She couldn't be jealous, could she? No, I doubted that. She hasn't once acted like she wanted to be friends with me. Maybe she was used to people leaving her for other friends.

Before I could protest, she continued, "I get it, I'm a freak. But I'm also a really good detective. I don't need help. I don't need friends. What I *do* need is to solve this case and not have to be your babysitter."

The train came to a stop and Shelby got off. I stood there stunned. I couldn't believe she would think that of me. *And* that she would abandon me on the subway.

"Watson," she called out from the subway doors, "this is your stop."

I quickly jumped out of the train as the warning bell rang out. My mind kept reeling with things to say to her. Did I want to be friends with Shelby? Or was I just using her? I remained mute as she walked me to the Columbia University Medical Center building where I had my doctor's appointment, with four minutes to spare. She didn't even turn around as I called after her once again to thank her. Never had someone so openly dismissed me as a friend.

She had been pretty clear since I met her that I was a bit of a nuisance to her.

Well, if she didn't want to be my friend, I was going to focus on making new friends. Zane was cool. I was going to meet a ton of people when school started. Yep, that was it. Starting tomorrow, I was going to study maps of the neighborhood and start getting around on my own. I was going to meet new people. I was going to become independent. I was going to be just fine on my own.

But then why did I feel so bad?

CHAPTER

10

"JOHN?"

Mom was waving her hand in front of my face as we walked around our new neighborhood that evening.

"Is everything all right?" she asked as she took my hand to walk across the street, just like she used to when I was little. "You seem distracted."

"Yeah, no," I mumbled, trying to regain a sense of normalcy after my bizarre afternoon.

I felt horrible after I left Shelby. *Was* I just using her? Yes, I needed her help since I was new to the city, but I kinda liked hanging out with her, too. She was just so . . . *different.* And I meant that in a good way. There was never a dull moment, that was for sure. And yeah, the case was interesting. How could I resist investigating a dognapping?

But I also knew that I needed to find some new friends. Some guys. People who would *want* to be friends with me.

"How did the rest of your day go?"

"Fine," I replied.

"Just *fine?*" She mimicked my monotone response back to me.

I was usually chattier with Mom, but I really didn't know what to say. I couldn't let her know about the case since she wouldn't approve of my running around the city with a relative stranger. But the case was all that was on my mind. And Shelby.

"Oh my," Mom said under her breath, and she steered us clear of Billy as he rummaged through the garbage. "So sad."

I looked down, not wanting him to recognize me since Mom would not be okay with the fact that I apparently associated with dudes who went through the trash.

Mom began going through her purse. "I know you shouldn't give homeless people money directly, but it's so hard to watch someone starve."

Just then, Billy lifted his head up. "Hey! I know you!" He pointed at me, and I could sense Mom tense up. She zipped up her purse and held it tighter to her body. "You're Shelby's friend, right?"

I nodded in response, ignoring Mom's horrified stare.

"You tell her all's well in the neighborhood! Nothing to report."

"Sounds good," I replied as I picked up my pace, but I couldn't walk too fast, as Mom still had a slight limp from her injury.

"You know him?" Mom asked with wide eyes.

"Shelby does, he's a freegan—he only eats food that's thrown out," I explained.

Mom looked back at him with a surprised glance. She then laughed lightly. "Only in New York!"

She had no idea.

I tried to remember everything Shelby had told me about our neighborhood. When I walked with Shelby, so many people said hello to her, but now everybody rushed by without even glancing up at Mom or me. The neighborhood didn't seem as friendly.

"This is the pizzeria I was telling you about," I said as we stopped in front of Sal's. The menu was placed in the window

next to photos of Sal with a bunch of politicians, athletes, and celebrities who had eaten there.

Mom tilted her head and pointed toward a photo up in the corner. "Isn't that Shelby?"

Sure enough, there was a photo of a beaming Sal with his arm around Shelby, who appeared put out by the attention.

"Is she a local celebrity or something?" Mom asked with an amused tone in her voice.

"Or something," I replied, knowing that as much as Shelby seemed not to enjoy that photo, I was positive her ego felt otherwise.

"Well, I'm hungry. Let's go in!"

We entered the narrow pizzeria, which had a long counter that contained numerous large pizzas behind a glass partition. Against the opposite wall were booths with red-and-white-checkered tablecloths. My mouth began watering as the smell of pizza, garlic, and melted cheese wafted from the brick oven in the back.

Mom and I slid into an empty booth directly across from the air conditioner, which was blasting. My eyes darted around the large menu, wondering if I should get pasta or pizza. It was always a treat when Mom let me eat whatever I wanted. Granted, it meant that she would insist on monitoring my glucose levels and personally administering my nightly insulin shot, but it was worth it.

"I think we have to get a pizza, right?" Mom smiled at me. "When in New York City . . ."

Sal came up to our table and placed a plate of garlic knots in the center.

"We didn't order these," Mom began to explain, before Sal cut her off.

"Any friend of Shelby's is a friend of mine!" He patted me on the back before running behind the counter to help a couple who walked in. I didn't even have a chance to tell him that Shelby only considered me to be a pain.

"Is there anybody in this neighborhood who doesn't know Shelby?" Mom asked.

"I don't think so." I took a bite of the greasy bread, and my eyes nearly rolled back into my head at the perfect blend of butter and garlic.

"Whoa," Mom commented before taking a bigger bite.

It was possible we devoured the entire plate in record time. Luckily, Sal took our pizza order while another guy delivered our drinks—iced tea for Mom, water for me (because it didn't matter the occasion; I was never allowed to drink soda).

"What are you up to tomorrow?" Mom asked.

I had no idea what was going to happen tomorrow. I was on my own. Which was exciting and also completely scary.

"Well, I have more boxes to unpack."

"John"—Mom's brow furrowed—"I told you to do that today. I know it's not fun, but I need your help. It's just you and me now. Will you please finish tomorrow?"

"Yes, I'm really sorry." I hated that I'd let her down. But if we were really staying here, why did it matter how long it took to unpack? "I was going to finish this afternoon, and then, well, Shelby and I met up with one of her friends."

Okay, that was a lie, since Shelby doesn't have friends (present company included).

"I felt a bit cooped up and wanted to meet some new people."

Mom reached out and grabbed my hand. "I know exactly what you mean. I'm glad you're making friends."

I kept forgetting that this was a new place for Mom, too. She had to start over just like me.

Honestly, making friends had never been a problem for me. But I was worried New York City was going to be different. There were so many options of places to go and people to meet—what if I got lost in the shuffle?

Mom cleared her throat and looked down at the table. I instantly knew what was coming next. "So, I finally reached your father today."

I twisted the napkin in my lap. "How is he?"

I hadn't spoken to Dad since we moved. We kept missing each other. For three days. *Three days*. It was the longest I'd gone without talking to him. I knew it was going to be hard living so far away from him, but I figured we'd always be able to talk. But so far, nothing.

"He's good. He's going to call tonight around eight." Mom's jaw tightened. "He promised."

I nodded as I took another slice of pizza. I didn't want Mom to know how much it upset me that she needed to remind him to call. He should *want* to talk to his own son.

"How are you doing?" she asked.

I shrugged my shoulders as I focused on chewing my food, trying to swallow away my hurt.

"John?" she prodded. "This has been a tough transition for him as well—we're all adjusting."

Was she defending him? Like, really, Mom?

When she realized I wasn't in the mood for this talk or defending Dad, she decided to change the subject.

"So Shelby!" Mom said with a laugh.

Ugh. Wrong topic. Sure, let's go from talking about your father who doesn't want to talk to you, to the girl who doesn't want to be your friend.

I'd never felt so alone.

Mom didn't seem to notice my discomfort. "You seem to be getting pretty tight with her. Why am I not surprised that you've taken her under your wing?" Mom said with a proud smile. "You really like hanging out with her?"

I looked up at Mom. It was such a simple question, wasn't it? Did I like hanging out with her?

Well, it was complicated.

Shelby could be extremely rude, temperamental, and

prickly—and that was putting it mildly. (No wonder she didn't have any friends.)

But then I thought about all the things I'd learned and been exposed to from knowing her for only a couple days.

Actually, the answer was pretty simple.

"Yeah, I do." But the more I thought about Shelby, the more I came to my own deduction about her. She was so uncomfortable today when she had to pretend to be a friend. Being friends with someone should be second nature. I never really thought about it. I was just myself around my friends. But I've had years of practice. Shelby didn't have any. She might be smart, but she didn't know any better.

This thought kept nagging at me. Maybe it was so easy for her to dismiss me because she never had anybody ever *want* to be her friend before.

"Mom, I think she needs my help."

Yeah, Shelby didn't need my help solving a case, but I couldn't shake the feeling that she needed someone to help in other ways.

Maybe what Shelby Holmes truly needed was a real friend.

CHAPTER
11

I THINK THIS GOES WITHOUT SAYING, BUT THINGS WEREN'T going that well for me.

I felt even worse the next morning as I waited outside for Shelby with a peace offering. I stood facing the front door, so she couldn't plan an escape.

"What do you want?" she asked with a scrunched face.

I waved a white tissue in one hand while I held the other out to her. She was about to walk right on by me when she paused. She looked at what was in my hand. "Is that for me?"

"It is." I gave her a bag of assorted candy that Kristos told me was her favorite. "It's a thank-you for yesterday. And an apology for making you leave the Lacys' early. And well, I know you think you don't need help—"

"I *know* I don't need help," she insisted. Her head suddenly tilted at me. Then she narrowed her eyes as she looked me up and down.

Oh no. She was doing her thing *to me*. I immediately

tensed up, not wanting to hear whatever she had to say. Especially since there wasn't anything she was going to tell me about myself that I didn't already know, I hoped.

Her scowl softened slightly. "This long of a verbal sabbatical with your father must be arduous."

She knew. Of course she knew. (At least I think I knew what she was talking about.)

Dad didn't call last night. I sat, like a total chump, with Mom's phone on my lap, waiting for his call. When he was ten minutes late, Mom grabbed her phone and locked herself in her room, and I could hear her leaving messages, her voice getting louder with each one.

His response? Zip. Zilch. Nada. Diddly-squat.

Maybe I should hire Shelby to solve the case of the disappearing dad?

"We don't have to talk about it," Shelby offered.

So Shelby *could* read social cues.

I didn't want to talk about it. I didn't want to even think about it. It was too painful. What I *did* want was to get back to this case. I needed something to distract me. Something that would make me feel useful.

"Thanks." I stood up a little straighter, hoping to appear more confident. "Listen, it's obvious you don't need my help solving the case, but I figured that maybe I could help you deal with the Lacys. They seem like a handful."

It was the only thing I could think of to get her to agree to let me help her—to make the Lacys seem like the problem.

Shelby paused for a moment. She untied the bag and put a few Swedish Fish in her mouth. After a few moments of consideration (and chewing), she finally said, "They have proved to be rather troublesome. With such dissonance amongst them, I wouldn't have blamed Daisy for running away."

I debated saying more but realized it was best to leave my argument as basic as possible.

Shelby took another handful of candy. My teeth hurt just watching her inhale all that sugar.

She nodded. "Fine, but at no point are you to impede my investigation."

"Of course!" I replied, even though I wasn't sure what *impede* meant. I figured it was her way of telling me to stay out of her way.

"Yes!" I threw my fist in the air, excited that I was able to go back to the Lacys' and figure out what happened to Daisy.

Shelby shook her head. "Thank you, Watson, for the candy . . . and for making me already regret my decision."

An hour later, we were in the elevator on our way up to the Lacys' apartment. Shelby informed me on our subway ride that her goal for the day was to examine the apartment and make an official list of suspects, which currently included the five family members, even Tamra.

As we knocked on the front door of the apartment, I felt nerves in the pit of my stomach. I didn't know anything about solving crimes, but I planned on sticking close to Shelby to figure out how she did it.

"Hi, Shelby and John," Mrs. Lacy said after opening the door. She looked exhausted.

"Any word on Daisy?" Shelby asked.

Mrs. Lacy shook her head. "Nothing. As you can imagine, it was a rough night."

The three siblings were sitting in the living room. Zareen sat with a scowl on her face next to Zane, her arms folded. Mrs. Lacy sat next to Tamra, who sported bloodshot eyes. "Shelby, Tamra informed me that you're known around school as a bit of an amateur detective."

"There's nothing *amateur* about what I do," Shelby said to the shock of Mrs. Lacy (okay, and me—who would talk to an adult like that?).

"Ah," I interrupted in an attempt to make peace (yeah, *the Lacys* were the real problem), "we're simply here to help, Mrs. Lacy. Shelby has solved a bunch of crimes, so she's the best person for the job. You should see the respect she has in our neighborhood. She's like a celebrity!"

Shelby slowly turned toward me. I was waiting for her to make some snide comment or put me in my place, but she simply turned back to the family.

"We'll take all the help we can get," Mrs. Lacy continued. "What do you need from us?"

Shelby got right down to it. "It would be helpful if you could each tell me where you were the morning Daisy went missing."

"I was here the whole time," Zareen stated quickly. "I didn't leave. Ask security!"

Hmm. She seemed pretty agitated. And really insistent that she was innocent. Anytime I watched a cop show, it was usually the guilty people who were the most annoyed at being questioned.

Zane went next. "I went to play some ball with my boys, around eight. I didn't see or hear Daisy or Roxy before I left. I went straight to the courts over at the Great Lawn. I had no idea Daisy was missing until Tamra called me. I think that was about two hours later."

"Okay. Mrs. Lacy?"

"I was at a seven a.m. Pilates class. I didn't see either dog before I left. I assumed they were in the dog room. Ed left for work at the same time. It wasn't until I got back that we knew she was missing."

Shelby walked over and studied each member of the

family. Each person shifted uncomfortably when it was their turn. Honestly, they all looked guilty, although I would've probably acted the same way during one of Shelby's examinations.

"Mrs. Lacy, how often is the laundry done in the house?" she asked.

"Almost every day. With five people, we go through a lot of clothes."

"I see." Shelby was pacing back and forth. "So it is more than likely that you are each wearing a clean set of clothes."

"Yes," Mrs. Lacy replied while the others nodded.

"And are the dogs allowed on the furniture?"

"No."

Where was she going with this?

"And I'm assuming the floors are cleaned regularly?"

"Yes, with two dogs, we try to keep the place clean. What does—"

But before Mrs. Lacy could finish her question, Shelby knelt down in front of Zareen.

"Hey!" Zareen protested as Shelby seemed to pinch her leg. "What are you doing?"

Shelby held up something that I couldn't see from across the room. "Roxy is a black-haired dog. I believe this is a white dog hair, is it not?"

The three other Lacys stood up quickly and examined the piece of hair.

"Could you please tell us, Zareen: if you're wearing a new outfit and the house is regularly cleaned for dog hair, how is it that you have a piece of hair that appears to match Daisy's?"

Zareen's mouth fell open. "I—I—I . . ." she stammered.

"I KNEW IT!" Tamra got in her sister's face. "YOU DID IT!"

"I didn't!" Zareen protested. "I was at the dog park this morning! There were other dogs everywhere! That's probably where it came from!"

"Girls, we discussed this: no more fighting, please," Mrs. Lacy begged. "Zareen, honey, if you know anything about Daisy's disappearance, you have to tell us. You won't get in trouble. We only want her back."

A tear began rolling down Zareen's cheek. "I can't believe you don't believe me. I didn't take her."

Zane hugged his twin. "It's okay, Lil' Z. I believe you."

Zane had to believe his own sister, although Zareen's case wasn't looking good. I couldn't help but feel a little bad for her since she was crying and her own mother basically accused her of stealing Daisy. If it wasn't Zareen, who else could it have been?

"I didn't do it," Zareen said in a small voice.

Everybody looked over at Shelby.

"Do you have anybody who witnessed that you were at the park this morning? Preferably someone with a white-haired dog."

Zareen nodded, but then everybody's attention went to something behind me.

"Where on earth have you been?" Mrs. Lacy asked, desperation in her voice.

I turned around and saw an older white guy with black hair that was graying around his temples. While this was the first time I'd ever seen this dude, I wasn't going to ignore the large piece of evidence in his hands: Roxy, who was as quiet as could be.

Maybe there was someone else who could've taken Daisy.

CHAPTER 12

"WE'VE BEEN TRYING TO REACH YOU ALL DAY YESTERDAY and this morning! Daisy's gone missing!" Mrs. Lacy threw her hands up in the air in frustration.

"What?" the man replied as Roxy licked his hand, as happy as she could be in his arms.

Tamra and Mrs. Lacy gave him the basics while Zane filled Shelby and me in: this man was Theo Emerson, Daisy's trainer. He'd been away because of a family emergency involving a sick aunt but had been due to arrive back that morning. They hadn't heard from him all week.

"She couldn't have gone far," Emerson said as he placed Roxy on the floor. Roxy, in turn, ran right up to Shelby and me and started barking fiercely.

At least everybody was now aware that *we* couldn't have taken Daisy.

Zareen picked up Roxy and took her out of the living room while Shelby approached the trainer and studied him intently.

"I'm sorry. I don't believe I've met your friends." The trainer nodded to us and seemed unnerved that Shelby was only inches away from him.

"Hello, I'm Shelby Holmes," she stated. "If you dab a washcloth in some cooled Earl Grey tea, it will help with your sunburn."

It was then that I realized his nose and cheeks were rather red and peeling. The rest of him was tan, which wasn't surprising, since it was the end of summer.

"Yes, well, I was . . ." he muttered as he took a step away from Shelby.

"Then again, Cozumel is quite sunny this time of year, isn't it?"

"I—I—I wouldn't know." He looked guiltily around the room. "I've never been."

"My mistake," Shelby said, even though I doubted she was ever mistaken. I knew she was setting a trap, and I couldn't wait for him to fall for it. "Do you mind if I ask where you acquired your necklace? I believe it's black coral."

The trainer reached up and touched a black necklace that was peeking out of his white button-down shirt. "This necklace?"

"Yes, that would be the exact necklace I'm referring to," Shelby stated drily.

"Oh, it was a gift. I've had it forever."

"I think it looks great on you," Tamra commented. "Although I don't think I've ever seen you wear it before."

Another clue! He was obviously lying. This trainer had to have taken Daisy. Roxy hadn't barked at him. Plus, he was mysteriously "out of town" all week.

Maybe I wasn't so bad at this sleuthing stuff.

Shelby got up close to Emerson—she only came to his elbow. "Do you happen to have video of Daisy on your phone? I'd like to see her in action, please." Shelby looked up and batted her eyelashes at this guy.

He had no clue this seemingly sweet little girl was setting him up (okay, maybe Shelby wasn't that bad of an actress after all).

"Sure." He reached into his pocket and pulled out his phone. Shelby got on her tiptoes, and her face was only a couple of inches away from the screen as he brought up a video of Daisy competing in her last show.

"What an amazing creature! Do you train other dogs competing on Saturday?"

"While I do train others, Daisy's the only dog I have on Saturday. Instead of sitting around watching videos, why aren't we doing something to find her?" He shoved his phone back in his pocket.

"That's exactly what we're doing," Mrs. Lacy stated

tersely. "Nobody in security saw her leave the building yesterday morning, so she must be somewhere nearby. Shelby is here to help, as is her friend John."

"You know," Shelby interjected, "I'm sure you want to catch up with Mr. Emerson, so Watson and I will go in the room next door to give you some privacy."

I couldn't believe Shelby was going to leave the room when the trainer was certainly guilty . . . of something. Of what, I wasn't sure, but Shelby would know.

"Thank you, Shelby," Mrs. Lacy said as the group sat down.

Shelby turned to leave, then tripped and went flying forward, knocking the trainer to the floor.

Just when I thought she knew what she was doing . . .

"I'm so, so sorry!" Shelby exclaimed as she reached her hand down to the trainer to help him back to his feet. "I'm such a klutz. I'm just glad I didn't break any valuables or a limb!" She then laughed so hard she snorted. "Silly me!"

The trainer stared at her with his mouth slightly open, probably in shock that such a tiny person could knock him down.

"Sorry, again!" Shelby called after the group as we retreated to the adjacent TV room.

"What was that all about?" I asked when we finally were out of earshot.

Shelby slowly turned around and held out something in her hand.

It was the trainer's phone.

CHAPTER 13

"YOU *STOLE* HIS PHONE?" I ASKED A BIT TOO LOUDLY.

"Shh!" Shelby brought the screen to life and put in a four-digit password. "I'm merely borrowing it for the sake of my investigation. I'll return it once I am satisfied with the evidence I'll no doubt obtain."

That's why she asked to see the footage. She was certainly close enough to see his password.

Mental note: if Mom ever lets me get a cell phone, don't use it anywhere near Shelby Holmes.

"Hello! What's this?" Shelby exclaimed as she started scrolling through photos of the trainer on a beach with a younger blonde woman. "He was in Cozumel, and just yesterday. I knew it. Granted, he could've acquired black coral in Hawaii or New Zealand, but since he was only gone for a few days, Mexico seemed most likely."

"Is there anything you don't know?" I blurted out. I'd

never heard of black coral, let alone know where it could be purchased.

"It's important to be well-rounded if you want to catch somebody in a lie."

Another mental note: never lie to Shelby Holmes.

"Here's my question for you, Watson." She pulled up a photo of the trainer at a candlelit dinner with the same woman. "How can a dog trainer afford such an expensive vacation? This is an all-inclusive resort, which isn't cheap, although it is August, so not peak season for Mexico, but still. His clothes also told me that he doesn't have a lot of expendable income: his shoes were significantly worn; the cuffs on his pants were tattered. Plus, he was with a much younger woman. She's in her early thirties while he's in his late fifties, divorced, has a couple kids, probably has to pay child support. Yes, he certainly isn't telling us the truth."

"He doesn't sit well with me, either," I confessed. "But if he's Daisy's trainer, what would he have to gain by stealing her? Wouldn't he make more money training a winning dog?"

"It depends on who he's betting on."

I couldn't help but laugh. "You mean, like, *gamble*? Do you really think that people gamble on a dog show? I mean, come on!"

"Well, there's really only one way to find out."

Before I had a chance to ask her how she was going to do that, Zane came into the room. "I can't take much more of this missing-dog drama. And you have to believe me when I say that there's no way Zareen took her. Just no way. I know her better than anyone, and she didn't do it."

Maybe Zane was right. Yeah, just a couple minutes ago, I was convinced it was Zareen. But now we had the trainer, who'd been caught in a lie. It was crazy how quickly things could change in this investigation (and in life).

Shelby, however, didn't seem swayed either way by Zane. "We shall see where the facts lead us."

"Do you really think you can find Daisy? Because I know if you do, Zareen's innocence will be proven."

Shelby nodded. "Of course I'll find Daisy." She said it like it was a fact. But we hardly had any evidence to tell us who took Daisy, let alone where she was being held.

"I hope so." He slumped down on the couch next to Shelby.

"So where do you play ball?" I asked. As much as I was enjoying this case and watching Shelby work, I wasn't going to waste an opportunity to make a new friend, especially a guy friend.

Most of my friends back on the post were guys. I liked being around other dudes. No offense to girls, but my guy friends were always a little more chill. There was no judgment. There were no expectations. My old buddies and I would just play some ball, watch some movies, and hang. I missed that. I really wanted that again. The only people I knew here were Mom, Shelby, and Mrs. Hudson.

I so needed to hang with some dudes.

"We play over in the park," Zane answered. "You should join us sometime."

"Yeah, that'd be cool. Thanks." I tried to be cool.

"You know"—Zane turned his attention to Shelby—"I like Emerson and all, but it bothers me that we've been trying to get ahold of him for over a day and he's been unreachable."

See! Even Zane thought the trainer did it.

Shelby's head jerked as if something had snapped into place in her head. "Interesting. Tell me, you're a year older than Zareen?" She moved forward so she was practically on top of Zane.

He leaned back into the couch cushions with an alarmed look on his face. "Uh, no, I'm fourteen minutes older than her. We're twins. What does that have to do with anything?"

"Simply curious," Shelby stated coolly.

"Well," Zane said as he got up from the couch (before Shelby could fall over him), "I better check in to see if there's anything I can do. Please find her, Shelby."

"I will."

He took a few steps but then stopped and put his hand in his pocket. "What on earth?" He pulled out the trainer's phone.

I stared at Shelby, who looked blankly back at Zane.

How did she get it in his pocket?

The close call on the couch now made sense.

Zane shook his head as he walked away. "Here I thought this day couldn't get any more bizarre."

Yeah, me too.

Shelby stayed quiet with her eyes closed until Tamra appeared back in the living room. It didn't take a face expert to tell that she'd been crying. "I don't understand why you're not interrogating Zareen. She clearly did it."

"She is a suspect, yes," Shelby admitted. "But *clearly* is not a word we can use at this juncture. There are too many elements in play." She then stood up. "Tamra, I think it's time you take me to the scene of the crime."

·CHAPTER·
14

THIS WAS CRUEL. I CERTAINLY HOPED IT WAS ALSO UNUSUAL.

The dog room off the foyer in the main hallway was twice the size of my bedroom at our new home. I was also pretty sure that the two dog-sized couches and beds probably cost more than all the furniture in our apartment combined.

Shelby dropped down to her knees and started climbing around, talking to herself as she inspected every dog toy, bowl, and chew stick.

"Is anything missing?" Shelby asked as she scratched behind her ear. (She was taking this whole putting-herself-in-the-victim's-shoes act a tad too far.)

"I don't think so," Tamra replied.

"What about the stuffed bone? You said that Daisy took her favorite toys—the stuffed Chihuahua and a stuffed bone—with her to bed. Caruso was in the hallway being chewed on by Roxy that morning and is over there in the corner. I didn't see a stuffed bone in your room or in this room. Where is it?"

Tamra started searching around the space. "You're right. It's missing!"

Shelby groaned loudly. "Honestly, do I have to do everything here? I asked you to tell me everything that happened, yet you failed to notice that one of Daisy's favorite toys was also missing."

"I—I . . ." Tamra broke down in tears. "I'm sorry. All I want is my dog back."

"Well, you aren't really helping by omitting such important and obvious facts from my investigation," Shelby stated flatly.

"Hey," I said in a low voice as I patted Tamra's back. "It's okay. There are so many toys in here I can see how you didn't realize it was missing."

"You're not helping, either, Watson," Shelby reprimanded me.

"Come on, Shelby, give us a break." I tried to reason with her. "Not everybody is a supersleuth like you. It's not fair to think that anybody can compete with your powers of observation. There's no need to lash out."

"You think *that* was lashing out?" Shelby snorted before returning to her four-limbed investigation of the area. *"Please."*

"Hey!" Zane walked into the room. "It's going to be okay, Tamra." He wrapped his arms around his sister, who continued to sob.

Zane turned his attention to Shelby, who was currently climbing into the canopy dog bed. "Ah, John, does she always do strange stuff like this?"

I could only shrug my shoulders in response since, in the limited time that I'd spent with Shelby, she'd been *exactly* like this.

Shelby jumped up and went over to the shelves that contained the dog food. "This is what they eat?"

"Yes," Tamra answered as she wiped away her tears. "They only eat organic dog food, and Miss Eugenia cooks chicken or wild salmon for them every night."

The dogs even ate better than me. Man, life in New York City wasn't fair.

Tamra approached the clear plastic containers that held the dog food. She patted the one that had the letter *D* in pink cursive. "This one's Daisy's."

"Thanks for clarifying," Shelby replied sarcastically.

I shot her a warning glance. If this was how she handled a client, I'd hate to see how she treated the thief once he (or she) was caught.

"Listen, Shelby." Zane put his hands in his pockets. "I'm willing to do whatever you need to help. We've got to find Daisy."

"Of course." Shelby stood up and placed her hand on Zane's shoulder. "You're the big brother. That's incredibly generous of you."

Wait a second. Why was Shelby being so nice to Zane? I'd never seen her be . . . normal to anyone.

Maybe she actually listened to me when I told her to take it easy?

"So, where do you go to school?" she asked. "You're not with us at the Academy."

"No, I'm not really into arts. I go to Saint Francis and play ball there."

"And what ball position do you perform?"

What now?

"I'm the point guard." Zane stood up a little straighter. "Basically, I'm the captain of our team."

"Are you really?" Shelby shook her head as if she was enamored by what Zane was saying. "That's quite an impressive feat."

"Yeah, I do all right."

Shelby then grabbed his hands and started examining them. "I presume you need to have strong hands to play the ball."

Now everybody in the room was staring at Shelby like she had lost her mind.

"CAN WE PLEASE GET BACK TO THE MATTER OF MY MISSING DOG?" Tamra screamed.

Shelby looked blankly at her. "But that's precisely what I'm doing."

"Really? Because it seems like you're flirting with my brother," Tamra shot back.

YES! That was what Shelby was trying to do, wasn't it?

Gross!

I had to cover my mouth so nobody could tell that I was holding back a laugh. Here I thought I'd seen it all, and then Shelby attempted to flirt with Zane. So there were now two things Shelby wasn't an expert on: flirting and friendship.

Shelby ignored Tamra's comment. "Who has keys to the apartment?"

Zane replied, "All of the family, Emerson, Eugenia, our cook, and Karina, the maid. Security also has a set, but they would only let in an authorized person who already has keys."

"And they would have a list downstairs of who's been allowed in?"

"Yes, but they already said that no one was spotted with Daisy that morning."

Shelby thought for a second. "I know Roxy barks at Eugenia—what about Karina?"

Zane laughed. "I mean, yeah, especially since she can't stand the vacuum."

"The better question would be who or what *doesn't* that dog bark at?" Tamra stated with a smirk.

"And who in the family does she bark at? You mentioned your father yesterday."

Tamra nodded. "Sometimes she barks at him, mostly when he's yelling at Zareen about Roxy. So *all the time*."

"Come on, Tamra." Zane folded his arms. "Roxy isn't that bad. Zareen does the best she can with him—give her a break."

"Why should I? She's the one who took Daisy!"

Not this again! Fortunately, Shelby stepped in before another meltdown could happen.

"I would love to see the list of visitors from the past week. Plus, it would be helpful if I could personally speak to security."

A thought suddenly hit me. Whenever I saw a movie set in fancy buildings like this, there were always all these cameras in the elevator and hallway. "Is there video footage of the elevator?"

"Yeah, but security already looked at it." Tamra looked sad. "They didn't find anything."

Shelby gritted her teeth. "You're telling me that there's been *security footage* this entire time and you neglected to mention it to me?"

Did I really think of something before Shelby? I mean, security footage seemed pretty obvious. Although I just thought of it now.

"But security didn't see Daisy on the footage."

"I don't care what security thinks they did or didn't see. I need to look at it with my own eyes."

Tamra seemed defeated. "Okay, let me go ask."

Zane followed Tamra out, while I felt pretty proud of myself for helping Shelby. For once.

Shelby looked me up and down. "Well, Watson, I have to hand it to you. That was rather . . . enlightening."

"Why, thank you!" I had a goofy grin on my face, which Shelby chose to ignore. She wasn't going to get off the hook so easily. "So what was that all about?"

"Are you referring to my slight mental lapse?" She was visibly frustrated that she hadn't thought of the footage first.

"No, I'm talking about you and Zane."

"I was simply inquiring about his extracurricular activities. Isn't that the same thing you've been annoying me with for the last two days?"

"No, you were flirting!" I pointed at her accusingly.

"Please," she said with a scowl. "However, I do have a question for you. In which sporting activity does one play the position of a point guard?"

"Are you serious?"

"I am extremely serious. Detective work isn't something to take lightly, Watson."

"Okay, but it's not like you've never heard of basketball. Right?"

"Basketball." She swirled the word on her tongue like she was speaking a foreign language. "And that's a sport that's played on a . . ."

"Court! A basketball court."

"So that was the 'ball' that you and Zane have been conversing about?"

"Yes." I rattled my head back and forth in an attempt to make this insane conversation make sense. "Do you really not know anything about basketball?"

"Why would I?"

"But you know about sleepwalking drugs and black coral and the height at which people spray-paint!" I could hardly keep my voice in check.

"Yes, I like to keep myself informed about *important* things."

"Sports are important!"

"To some." She scrunched up her nose.

"So what do you want to know?" I liked that I finally knew more about something than her. I could use this in the future if she made fun of me for not knowing the currency of a particular country I'd never heard of or the sleep habits of some wild creature.

"You've told me enough," she said as she went back into the hallway. "And I hope to forget it as soon as possible. I mustn't take up space in my brain attic with useless knowledge."

Brain attic?

Okay, maybe Shelby Holmes wasn't a genius. She was plain nuts.

"So?" Shelby looked expectantly as Tamra and Zane entered the hallway.

"You can go look at the footage," Tamra informed us.

"Excellent!" Shelby clapped her hands together. A ringing noise came from her large backpack. "Ugh," she sighed as she took out a cell phone.

"You have a phone?" I asked.

"My parents wanted to place a tracking device on me. This was the compromise that we reached."

Shelby's parents were a lot smarter than she gave them credit for.

"This is Shelby Holmes," she answered impatiently. "I see. However, this is not a convenient time, as I'm in the middle of a very important case." Shelby's face pinched tightly as she listened to the person on the other end of the line, probably some business associate or contact or whoever else would be calling her. "While I appreciate your sentiments, I mustn't—No, I'm simply . . . But it's an urgent—" She stomped her foot on the ground, and a few of the vases near us rattled. "But, *Mooooom!*"

It was her *mom?*

After a few more protests, she threw her phone into her bag with a frown. "I, unfortunately, need to take a rain check on the surveillance video. But I'll be back tomorrow to view it."

Seriously? Now Shelby was the one who had to leave. Maybe I could watch the footage?

Zane looked at me. "You want to go hit the court, John?"

I couldn't believe it! I was going to finally hang out with Zane and play ball and do something normal.

"Sure, that'd be cool," I said with a little tip of my chin, attempting not to appear as desperate as I felt.

"Sorry, Watson." Shelby gave me a tight smile. "Unfortunately, you have to come with me. That call concerned you as well."

~·CHAPTER·~
15

TWO HOURS LATER, MOM AND I FOUND OURSELVES KNOCKING on the door to apartment 221B.

"Come in!" A woman with the same red hair as Shelby, but pulled back in a loose bun, answered the door. "I'm so glad you were able to join us for dinner."

"Thank you for inviting us," Mom said as she handed over a pie that just came out of the oven. Mom and Mrs. Holmes ran into each other in the hallway, and Shelby's mom invited us to dinner.

"Shelby! Come over and say hello to our guests!" Mrs. Holmes motioned to her daughter.

I tried really, really hard to not laugh. I did. But I couldn't help myself. It was too much: Shelby was in a floral dress with a bow in her hair and didn't appear to be very happy about it.

"Greetings and salutations," Shelby said with an exaggerated curtsy. "Welcome to our oh-so-humble abode."

The living room had the same layout as ours one floor

below: brick fireplace along one wall and a bay window looking out onto Baker Street. They had a green velvet sofa on one side and two leather armchairs on the other, with an oval coffee table stacked with books in between. Sir Arthur was sleeping in a corner.

Off the living room was an alcove that held a dining table, which led into the kitchen, and then there was a staircase leading up to another floor.

"Dr. Watson brought us some pie. Isn't that nice?" Mrs. Holmes straightened the bow in Shelby's hair, and Shelby swatted her hand away like her mother was a fly.

"What kind of pie?" Shelby asked as she squirmed away from her mother's preening.

"Apple. I hope you like it," Mom replied.

"Hello! Hello!" A tall, pale, and extremely thin man with hair that was nearly as white as snow came into the room. "I'm Charles Holmes. So glad you could join us, Dr. Watson and John."

"Please, call me Janice." Mom shook Mr. Holmes's hand. "Thanks for having us."

"Our pleasure!" He clapped his hands together. "And, John, I hear our little Shelby has taken you around the neighborhood. I hope she didn't get you into too much trouble. Unfortunately, if there's trouble, she seems to find it." He rubbed Shelby's head.

"Daaaad." Shelby took a few steps back, her arms folded defiantly.

"It was a great way to get to know the neighborhood," I replied. "Plus, we went to a classmate's apartment in this giant building. I'd never seen a place so big." I spent the entire time Mom was baking trying to describe the Lacys' home. I might have left out that it wasn't anywhere close to where we lived. And that it had the separate dog room. That would've been too harsh to describe to her in our tiny apartment.

Okay, truthfully, I didn't mention anything about the dogs at all. I wanted Mom to think that I was having a normal afternoon with normal people doing normal kid things. Not investigating a dognapping. I figured it wasn't really lying if I simply happened to omit certain details.

"What friend?" Mr. Holmes asked. "That's great that you're making friends, Shelly."

"It's Shelby, Father. How many times must I remind you of that, especially since you had given me that designation?"

Shelby stomped back into the kitchen, where the clattering of pans could be heard.

"Oh, the perils of raising a rambunctious daughter. She certainly keeps us on our toes!" Mr. Holmes said with a shake of his head. "Please make yourselves comfortable."

He gestured to the seating area, where Mom and I sat down. After taking our drink orders, he gave us a big smile before retreating to the kitchen.

"He seems really nice," Mom commented while we sat in silence, hearing the occasional noise from the kitchen.

Shelby approached us with a tray that had our drinks.

"Thanks, Shelby!" Mom said. "It's been very sweet of you to show John around."

"Not like I had a choice," she muttered under her breath.

"Sorry?" Mom tilted forward.

There was another crash in the kitchen. Mom stood up. "Let me see if I can help."

Shelby sat down on the couch, her legs swinging nearly a foot above the carpet.

"Is *he* one of our esteemed dinner companions?" A boy with the same pale complexion as Mr. Holmes, but with light blond hair, sat down next to Shelby. *Michael Holmes, I presume?*

"Affirmative," Shelby replied. "His mother is in the kitchen assisting the parental units."

"Good thing she has combat training," Michael scoffed.

"Hey, man, I'm John!" I leaned over to shake his hand.

Michael studied me with bored eyes before picking up a large book from the coffee table.

"As you can see, Watson, Michael is the personality of the family."

"I'm also the brains," he said with a crooked grin.

"You wish."

Michael finally looked over at me. "Don't let her pedestrian parlor tricks impress you. My sister is more on par with your basic street con artist than the real detectives she's so desperate to impress."

"And how many cases have you solved, Michael?" Shelby shot back at him.

He crossed his legs and went back to reading his book.

Well, one mystery was solved: weirdness runs in the family.

"Dinner is served!" Mr. Holmes came out of the kitchen holding a dish with chicken, with Mom behind him with a bowl of green beans.

"I was thinking that you could sit at the head of the table, Janice." Mrs. Holmes pulled out the chair. "I'll have Charles sit at the foot, while the children and I take the sides."

"Sounds lovely."

Mom sat down, while I sat to her left. Michael sat down next to Shelby without even a glance in our direction.

"Michael," Mrs. Holmes said as she placed a napkin in her lap, "please say hello to Dr. Watson."

"Hello to Dr. Watson," he echoed in a monotone voice.

An awkward silence fell as we passed the various dishes around the table.

"So," Mom began, always attempting to make the best out of any situation no matter how awkward it might be, "what grade are you going into, Michael?"

"I commence my studies at Columbia University in two weeks," he replied while never taking his eyes off the roll he was buttering.

"Really? How old are you?"

"Sixteen."

"That's quite impressive."

Michael snorted. "Well, I can't think of anything more torturous than high school."

"I can," Shelby replied with a delighted snicker.

"Shelby." Mrs. Holmes gave a warning nudge to her daughter.

"So, John!" Mr. Holmes decided to put the attention on me. "What grade are you going into?"

"He's—" Shelby started to reply before her dad cut her off.

"Now, now, Shelby. It's polite to let people answer questions about themselves. We all know about your talents, but I would like to hear from John."

Shelby slumped back in her chair and began gnawing on a drumstick.

Did that really work? Was it possible for Shelby Holmes to be tamed?

Mr. Holmes shook his head. "You know how it is, Janice, with kids. They think they know everything. But what are you going to do? Kids will be kids!" He laughed and my mom gave him a polite smile.

Ah, *no*. Shelby and Michael were not *kids being kids*. And I was pretty certain Shelby *did* know everything (well, except about basketball). But you had to hand it to Mr. Holmes for at least trying to discipline Shelby. That couldn't be easy. (Which may be the biggest understatement of all time.)

Over the course of the meal, Mom, Mr. and Mrs. Holmes, and I talked about a bunch of things: army posts, Harlem, the Academy, and Columbia University. Shelby and Michael stayed eerily silent, barely looking up from their food. They both seemed put out that their parents were so inquisitive.

"Michael, why don't you clear the dishes so we can serve the delicious pie that Dr. Watson has brought?" Mr. Holmes suggested. Shelby perked up once pie was mentioned. "Shelby, you haven't eaten a single one of your green beans."

(Okay, so this was the one instance when Shelby really was a *kid being a kid*, even if it was something as predictable as not wanting to eat your vegetables.)

Shelby used her fork to move around the green beans on her plate. "Because green beans are an affront to the culinary arts."

(Never mind, no *kid* would ever talk like that.)

"Now, young lady, we'll have none of that. No dessert unless you finish your vegetables."

I pinched my lips together to avoid laughing. Shelby always acted above everything. Even though she was tiny, I had to keep reminding myself that she was only nine. But now, faced with a plate of green beans, she was finally acting her age.

It was kind of refreshing.

Shelby sulked for a couple minutes before taking her fork and spearing every single green bean on her plate. She then shoved the whole thing into her mouth while plugging her nose.

Scratch that—she was acting *waaay* younger than her age. (And it was hysterical.)

"Shelby!" Her mom reprimanded her as bits of green bean were falling from Shelby's open mouth and back onto the plate.

Shelby replied with an overfull mouth. I wasn't sure what she was saying, but I think it was along the lines of "I'm doing what I'm told."

Michael stood over his sister, waiting for her plate to be cleaned before he finally, mercifully, took it away.

Shelby's entire focus was on the pie, as mom began to cut it. Once a slice was placed in front of her, she dived greedily in. However, the second she took a bite, her eyes became wide and she spit the contents out onto her plate.

"Shelby!" her parents scolded in unison, while Michael burst into laughter, his first display of emotion all night.

"How absurdly foolish of me!" Shelby replied quickly, and then began to giggle embarrassingly. "I've been so distracted by my case I didn't stop to think that you'd be bringing a sugar-free pie, Dr. Watson. My apologies. This was my reckless mistake." She reached into the center of the table and took the sugar and dumped nearly the entire container onto her plate before picking up her fork and diving right back in.

Mom was rendered speechless while Mr. and Mrs. Holmes appeared to be horrified. I had to cut them some slack. They had to raise Shelby. I couldn't imagine living with someone who could analyze your every move. It must've been exhausting.

"Shelby, did you say that you have a *case*?" Mom asked, once she fully recovered.

"Yes, I'm a detective."

"I'm sure the cops can sleep at night knowing Shelby Holmes is on the case," Michael said snidely.

"At least *I* contribute to society," Shelby replied defensively.

"Oh no!" Michael appeared to be scandalized. "Was there a library book that had been shelved out of order?"

"Amateur," Shelby said under her breath. "Mother and Father, I was thinking it would be utterly delightful if I could enter Sir Arthur into a dog show on Saturday. I figured it would be something different for me to do. My friend from school is also entering her dog. What do you think?"

"Really?" Mr. Holmes exchanged an excited glance with his wife. "I think it would be splendid for you to do that. And with a friend? Well done, Shelby!"

"Great!" She pulled out a piece of paper from her dress. "I need you to sign the registration form."

"Oh, well, we can do it later. After all, we have guests."

"It will only take a second." Shelby produced a pen and slid the paper under her mother's hand, keeping her hand placed firmly on the top of the paper.

"Well, I suppose," her mom said as she signed the form. "It's nice to see you take interest in something outside of sleuthing."

I tried to make eye contact with Shelby to get a sense of what she was up to. She might have thought I didn't know a lot, but I knew having Sir Arthur be part of the competition had *everything* to do with sleuthing.

Later that evening, Mom knocked on my door as I was writing in my journal. After months of not being able to write, my hand could hardly keep up with everything I had to say.

"Thanks again for unpacking all those boxes," Mom said as she sat next to me on my bed. "I'm sorry that I haven't been able to help that much. I'm looking forward to a weekend off to hang out with my son." She rested her head against mine. "I can see why you like hanging out with Shelby. She's something else, huh?"

"No kidding." We both laughed a little.

"What are these 'cases' that Shelby works on?"

"Cases?" I played dumb. "What do you mean, cases?"

Mom narrowed her eyes. She knew when I was keeping something from her. "Shelby mentioned she was a detective working on a case at dinner. According to Mrs. Hudson, she's apparently pretty good. I shouldn't be surprised with the reception she gets in the neighborhood."

"Yeah, I guess," I conceded.

"I know you haven't met that many people yet, but you will. I'm glad you've made a friend in Shelby, but I don't want you getting involved in any of these cases. It's never a good idea to stick your nose into other people's business."

Too late.

CHAPTER
16

THERE WAS A LOUD BANGING ON OUR FRONT DOOR THE following morning. When I looked through the peephole, I was a little surprised to see who was on the other side.

"Hey, Shelby!"

"I thought I would come get you so as not to inconvenience you with waiting for me outside." While she spoke with her usual attitude, she was scratching the back of her leg with her foot.

No way! Was Shelby nervous? She sure seemed it. I mean, she was being nice to me, so she had to be uncomfortable. I didn't want her to feel more self-conscious, so I didn't comment on her odd (yet totally welcomed) behavior. She wanted me to come along. This time.

"We're going to leave for the Lacys' now?" I asked.

"We require a quick detour first. I need to converse with a contact."

It was the first time she used *we*. Maybe my security

footage idea yesterday made her finally realize how helpful I could be.

"Yeah, let me change." I ran into my room and put on my favorite outfit for playing basketball, just in case Zane wanted to play a game later.

As I walked back into the living room, Shelby gave me a quick once-over. "Don't you look rather sporting."

"Thanks!" I said as I looked down at my mesh shorts and army tee.

"And you think *I'm* the one with the crush on Zane," she said with a snort.

We started walking uptown several blocks in silence. She turned us west, farther away from the busy avenues.

"So do you think Zareen or the trainer did it? The dog show's tomorrow," I reminded her, not like she needed it.

"I have my theories," she replied with a curl of the lips.

"Would you care to share them?"

"Not at the moment. I still need to work a few things out. I'm hoping that once I study the surveillance footage things will start to clear up."

"But security already looked at it."

"True, but *I* haven't been able to observe it. I need to figure out *how* Daisy got away. Security only said they didn't see Daisy in the footage. I'm looking for something else."

"What?"

"That has yet to be determined."

Even though she wanted me here, she wasn't being very open about what she knew or what she was planning. However, after watching Shelby force her mom to sign that paper last night to get Sir Arthur in the dog show, I knew she had something up her sleeve.

"What aren't you telling me?"

"About what?"

"About the dog show tomorrow." I decided to give her a taste of her own medicine. "I noticed when you gave your mom the registration form, you didn't simply hand it to her. You slid it with your hand covering the top part." I searched my brain for what that could've meant. She didn't want her mom to see the top . . . where you usually have to fill out your personal information. "So I'm guessing either you put a different name on the form or a fake address."

Shelby stopped in her tracks. "Well done, Watson!"

It was a miracle! I received an actual compliment from Shelby!

"There may be hope for you yet!"

And then she had to continue talking.

"So whose name did you put on there?" I asked.

"Well, there's where you come in, Watson. You seem to want to be involved in the case, so I have a task for you."

"Really?" I was excited I'd finally gained her trust.

"If the unforeseen happens and I can't locate Daisy before tomorrow morning, I will need you to do the very simple task of bringing Sir Arthur to the dog show while I continue to suss out potential suspects. It's important for both of us to have backstage access, but that's only on the off chance that I haven't recovered Daisy by the end of the day."

So basically, she wanted me to walk her dog. Guess I still had a ways to go before she'd consider me essential.

"Why didn't you simply forge the signature?"

"I apprehend criminals. I'm not one of them."

She might not be a criminal, but she had no problem lying to her parents.

"So my name's at the top?"

"Heavens no. I gave you an alias since all of Sir Arthur's papers are in my family's name. Tomorrow you'll be Sheldon Holmes."

"Sheldon?"

"Yes, by your tone, I take it you would've preferred a different moniker?"

While I like the name John just fine, as Shelby had already pointed out, so many people have that name. Zane was such an unusual name it stood out. If I was going undercover, I wanted a name like that.

"Why couldn't you have given me something cooler, like Shane or Spencer or Silas?" My mind blanked at more names.

Okay, maybe coming up with names was harder than I thought. "Or, I don't know . . . Sherlock."

"*Sherlock?*" Shelby scoffed. "What kind of name is *Sherlock*? You wanted to go undercover as *Sherlock Holmes*? Like anybody would believe that."

I ignored Shelby's snickering. Instead, I tried to remember every turn we'd taken so I could start getting around on my own. While I wanted to be here, having Shelby as a tour guide really grated on my self-esteem.

At first, we passed apartment complexes, but we were now walking by buildings that were abandoned and boarded up. The streets were mostly empty, except for the occasional homeless person. I began to get jittery whenever a horn or alarm went off. I practically jumped out of my skin when glass from a broken window shattered near us. What kind of contact did Shelby have who would live here?

"Ah, Shelby," I said as a rat scurried away from an empty lot that was filled with garbage. "This doesn't seem very safe."

"Oh, I would advise that you never come here alone. This isn't a very desirable part of town."

Then what were we doing there? And why did Shelby feel that she was invincible?

"Don't worry, Watson. We're almost there."

Oddly enough, that didn't make me feel better. I wanted to turn around and go back to our safe street. Or better yet,

the Lacys', which seemed like a million miles away from here instead of just a few.

A young guy, probably around sixteen, turned the corner. The second he spotted us, his eyes narrowed and a menacing grin appeared on his face. "Hold up." He walked over with a swagger. His jeans were hanging low on his hips; his Yankees cap sat crooked on his head. "What do you think you're doing here?"

Shelby wisely ignored him and kept walking.

"Yo! I'm talking to you!" He jumped in front of us.

My stomach filled with butterflies. I was used to military posts where only authorized personnel were allowed. I never had to worry about being mugged or whatever this guy was going to do. But Shelby didn't seem fazed.

Shelby sighed. "If you must know, I'm here to speak with Dante. You may escort us there if you feel the need. However, I am more than capable of making the journey unaccompanied."

The guy started laughing. "Oh, you think you've got some business with Dante?" Much to my dread, he turned to me. "And what about you? You some mute or something?"

My manly response was a terrified stare.

"You must be new," Shelby declared, then gave the guy a quick once-over.

Uh-oh. She was going to do that Shelby thing she did, and I had a feeling this guy was not going to appreciate it. If only I could've found my voice, or stopped my legs from shaking so I could've run away. I'm a pretty fast runner, and I bet this guy wouldn't have gotten very far before his pants fell down. But I didn't want to leave Shelby alone. As much as she was under the impression that she could take care of herself, I wasn't so sure.

Shelby began while I held my breath. "While I admire your attempt to get away from your white-collar roots, I can see through your act. Why don't you put your expensive shoes that your Wall Street banker father bought to use and walk away? Or does Dante not know that you only play dress-up during the summer and weekends when you don't have to attend your all-boys academy?"

The guy looked like he was going to be sick. "Who do you think you are?" he asked with his chin held high, but there was a waver in his voice.

"Someone who's finished having this conversation. Come on, Watson." Shelby sidestepped the guy and turned the corner, where there was a group of five other teens sitting on a park bench across the street, all of them bearing a resemblance to the guy we just left.

Great. Now we were in even bigger trouble. Shelby proved that she could handle one bully, but five?

"Why, if it isn't the great Shelby Holmes!" The guy in the center stood up as we approached. My jaw practically hit the floor. This guy not only knew Shelby, he looked happy to see her. "What's happening, World's Smallest Detective?" He held out his fist for Shelby to bump. After it was clear she was not going to appease him, he put it down.

"I need some information, Dante."

"Anything for you, Shelby." He turned to his companions, who seemed as perplexed as I was. "This little girl may be the smartest person you dudes will ever come across—she got me out of a jam a few months back. You see her around, you take good care of her. Am I clear?"

The group all gave Shelby a nod of respect.

Dante motioned over to me. "You got muscle now? Smart move, girl—you sure do make some enemies."

This guy was pretty smart.

"Dante, this is John Watson. He has moved into my building, and I'm showing him around."

Dante laughed. "These parts aren't usually on the tourist maps. Listen, John Watson, you need anything, you come to me, okay? Any friend of Shelby's is a friend of mine. Maybe in a few years, when you get a little older, you can come work for me."

I had no idea what this guy did, but I was fairly positive it was something that Mom would've had a huge problem with. I didn't want to be rude to one of Shelby's contacts, but I also didn't want to agree to a potential life in crime.

What had Shelby gotten us into?

"I don't think so, Dante." Shelby wagged her finger at him. "John Watson is going to be an accomplished writer, not a thug."

A chorus of *oooh*s came from the group. I highly doubted many people talked to Dante like that and got away with it, but he responded by laughing.

"What's this info you need?"

"Do you know if there's betting going on for the Manhattan Kennel Club Dog Show tomorrow—specifically, have there been any rumblings of someone trying to fix the toy breed competition?"

This guy was a *bookie*? I'd only seen bookies on TV. They were always really shady characters who threatened people who owed them money from a bet they'd lost. I couldn't believe Shelby would be friends with one.

Wait, Shelby Holmes didn't have *friends*; she had *contacts*.

I was a little scared, but also curious. (Okay, I was really scared. I mean, we were hanging out in this supersketchy place where I had no idea how to get home. Plus, if Mom ever found out, she'd really give me something to fear. Dante and his gang seemed tough, but they had nothing on my mom.)

The group erupted into laughter at Shelby's questions about the dog show. "Yo, Dante!" one of the guys yelled. "Put me down for a nickel on a poodle!"

"Shelby," Dante said with a grin, "I work with legitimate sporting events."

"There's nothing legitimate about what you do, Dante," Shelby fired back.

"All I'm saying is that I don't deal with silly things like dog shows. I don't know where you got your information that I did, but it was wrong."

Could it possibly be that Shelby was finally wrong about something? I looked up to the sky, waiting for the heavens to open up and flood the city.

"Am I really?" Shelby asked with a raised eyebrow.

"Fellas!" Dante motioned to the group. "Give me a second with Shelby and John Watson so I can educate them on what we do here."

The group began to disperse across the street. Dante waited until they were out of earshot before he leaned in and spoke softly. "You got some information that may affect my line?"

"What?" I blurted out. "You really do take bets on dog shows?"

"Shh, man!" Danted hissed. "I've got a reputation to uphold! Of course I take bets. Those rich folks love throwing money on their prized pooches. Last year I earned more green than I did during the NBA Finals!"

Unreal.

"I've got a missing dog." Shelby got back to business. "What do you think the chances are that a trainer would sabotage his front-runner to earn more money?"

"Which dog?"

"Daisy, the Cavalier King Charles spaniel that the Lacys own."

"Why would the trainer do that?" Dante scratched his head. "Unless the dog with the biggest odds won and he placed a ton of money, he'd be better off sticking with his own dog."

Shelby looked thoughtful for a moment. "Who do you have as the underdog?"

Both Dante and I chuckled at her unintentional pun.

"Let me see." Dante took out a small notebook from his back pocket and started flipping through pages. "I have Daisy as the favorite, but Mr. Wiggles is a close second. The dog that I have with the biggest odds is a Yorkshire terrier named Princess. First year showing. Also has a new trainer."

"Hmmm," Shelby considered his information. "It doesn't fit that Emerson would risk it."

Dante scribbled in his notebook. "So let me get this straight: Daisy will be a no-show tomorrow?"

"No." Shelby stood up straighter, looking defiant. "Daisy will be there."

I wanted to ask her how she knew that when there were so many open-ended questions and suspects. But I stopped myself, because I knew that if Shelby was certain of something, it wasn't without reason.

Shelby nodded at Dante. "Thank you for your help."

"Anytime, Shelby. You be careful—that's some shady business you're dealing in."

"And you're certainly an expert on that."

Dante began shaking his head as we walked away. "You're too much, Shelby."

"So I've been informed."

CHAPTER 17

SHELBY WAS QUIET DURING THE SUBWAY RIDE TO THE LACYS'. She wasn't one for small talk, so I studied all the people who got on and off the subway.

"You know, Watson, I have to admit that it's been quite helpful having you around," she finally said. "Sometimes nothing clears up a case more than stating the facts to another person. Perhaps I should reconsider my position on having an assistant."

Whoa. Whoa. Whoa. I didn't want to be anybody's *assistant.* Yeah, I could learn a lot from Shelby, but as an apprentice or something. NOT her assistant.

Was that why she wanted me here today? Not because she thought I could genuinely help her, but because she wanted me to be her assistant? Was I supposed to fetch her coffee or something? (More like keep her properly sugared.)

Before I could ask her to clarify my position, she launched into a recap of the investigation. "So let's look at the facts:

Daisy went missing sometime between midnight, when Mr. Lacy spotted Daisy in bed with Tamra as he checked in on all three kids before he went to sleep, and nine, when Tamra went downstairs and couldn't find her. Mr. Lacy was already at work, Mrs. Lacy was at an exercise class, Zareen was home, and Zane was in the park. While it is possible any one of them could've taken her, the security footage allegedly doesn't show Daisy leaving. We have a jealous older sister who sleepwalks and a trainer who is in need of money and was conveniently MIA when Mrs. Lacy tried to reach him when Daisy went missing."

"Sounds about right to me. So what's *our* next step?" I emphasized the *our* on purpose.

"I'm going to take another look around the house in case there are any new clues."

"New clues? You were pretty thorough." I was still having trouble getting the images of Shelby running around like a dog and her bum sticking up in the air out of my mind.

"It's clear that it's somebody who has access to the apartment. They may have gotten careless. Plus, I need to see that footage. That's going to explain how the culprit got away."

"What can I do?" *Please don't ask me to get you a candy bar.*

"I'm glad you asked, as I'd like to give you a little exercise."

An exercise? Seriously? It was summer, when I don't have to worry about stuff like, you know, homework.

The subway doors opened and Shelby gracefully weaved between the passengers waiting to get on the train while I kept bumping into everybody.

"I'd like you to not simply see, but observe everybody and everything today. Analyze body language. Observe. Remember everything and put it in your brain attic."

"Brain attic?" She mentioned that yesterday, but I had, yet again, no idea what she was talking about.

"I look at a brain like it's an empty attic," Shelby started to explain as we walked toward the Lacys'. "You decide how you're going to pack it. Am I going to waste precious real estate to fill it with useless knowledge like sporting terms? Of course not. I make sure to fill my attic only with memories and information that will best serve me as a detective. While most people's brains are a jumble of life events and random facts, I keep my brain well organized. I have different storage spaces that are for specific areas of expertise. For example, I have a whole storage space filled with geology facts, which is why I knew about the black coral. But nothing would ever get in my attic if I didn't observe and realize that I needed to remember it. When I first attempted this, granted I was quite young, being only four years old and all, I would say to myself '*This* I need to remember' to ensure that it wasn't something I'd forget."

This I really did need to remember.

My brain began throbbing, trying to take in everything she was telling me. She was rattling off so many specifics about ways to really observe, I could hardly keep up.

She did have a point, though: how many times have I hung out with someone or done something and then Mom asked me what I did and I said, "nothing." It wasn't because I didn't have anything to share with her, but I hadn't been paying close attention. I'd play some ball or watch a movie, but I never really felt present. Maybe that's because I knew I was only a year or two away from moving somewhere else. What was the point of trying to remember every detail of a friend or a home when it was going to go away and be replaced with a new one?

Mom promised me that we'd be here for a while. She had no plans to take us away from New York City anytime soon. I suppose this was as good a time as any to embrace what Shelby was telling me. Observe everything around me. Take it in. Remember.

Even though Shelby had her incredible brain storage unit, I had my journal. While I always focused on fiction, maybe I should start writing about living in New York City and perhaps even Shelby herself. Sure, I had taken notes about our first encounter and yesterday, but it was only the basics. I could really observe and then report it in detail.

DOG MISSING

Tri-color Cavalier King Charles Spaniel was taken from our loving home.

Daisy has white and black fur with brown on her face.

REWARD

for any information leading to the recovery of our beloved dog.

We turned the corner onto Central Park West to find Daisy's face everywhere. There were signs plastered on every streetlight, every empty wall space.

Reward? There was going to be money if we found Daisy? I hadn't even thought of that. I'd assumed Shelby worked for free pizza and sugar.

Shelby's nose scrunched as she studied the flyer. "Ye of little faith."

She shook her head as we crossed the street to the Lacys' building. "So you want me to observe everything I see today and remember it."

"That is the pedestrian version, but yes."

We entered the building, where even more flyers were posted. Security motioned us to go through to the elevators.

"Okay," I said, because I wanted to make sure I got everything right. I wanted to prove that I could also be a detective. "So do you want, like, a written report or something?"

"No, I have a feeling you're going to know if there's something to tell me."

I appreciated she had that kind of confidence in me. I hoped she was right. I wasn't exactly sure what she was expecting me to find. But I think she knew. It would've been nice if she could've just told me, but why would she make anything easy for anybody?

Tamra opened the door before we hardly had a chance to knock. "I'm so sorry, Shelby! Please don't get mad!"

"What did you do?" Shelby snapped at her.

"It's been over forty-eight hours. Dad finally caved. It's not that I don't trust that you'll find her, but—" Tamra's bottom lip started to tremble.

When we entered the apartment, Shelby let out a loud groan that made everybody's head turn in the living room.

"Well, hello there, Holmes."

"Detective Lestrade."

CHAPTER 18

SHELBY DRAGGED HER FEET TO THE LIVING ROOM, WHERE Lestrade was sitting on a couch next to Mrs. Lacy. "I see your career has gone to the dogs, Lestrade."

Lestrade glared at Shelby. "The Lacys were smart enough to know when the professionals should be involved."

"We appreciate all your help so far, Shelby," Mrs. Lacy admitted, much to the aggravation of Lestrade. "However, Detective Lestrade is doing us all a favor by being here."

"Anything for one of the police department's biggest donors." Lestrade gave Mrs. Lacy a big smile.

Ah, that was why Lestrade was here. I didn't think the police would've ever gotten involved in a case like this, but money talks. And the Lacys' money probably screamed.

"I hear you have some pretty far-fetched conspiracy theories, Holmes." Lestrade leaned back on the couch, a cup of coffee in hand. "It's pretty cut and dried—dogs wander off all the time."

"But Daisy would never do that!" Tamra protested.

"You've got the flyers posted around the neighborhood. I've got calls into the shelters around the city. Don't worry, she was probably already picked up and is safe at a nearby kennel."

"Yes, wonderful job, Detective Lestrade," Shelby said with a grimace. "Award-winning work. However, wouldn't whoever found her call the number on her collar?"

It was pretty obvious Lestrade didn't have any more information than we did. Probably less.

"Yes. Although we would've received a ransom call if she'd been dognapped," Lestrade volleyed back at Shelby.

"I never inferred that this was a dognapping."

"Then what would you call it?" Lestrade lifted an eyebrow, enjoying her attempt to aggravate Shelby.

Shelby replied by turning on her heel to leave the room.

"Where do you think you're going?" Lestrade called after her.

"To the dogs' room."

"Heading home so soon?" Lestrade said with a snicker as she took another sip of coffee.

Ouch.

I got that Shelby could be very grating and disrespectful and impatient and . . . but Lestrade was the adult and a professional. She shouldn't let Shelby get under her skin so much. Someone had to be the more mature of the two, and it really should've been the grown-up.

Shelby narrowed her eyes at the detective. I nudged her gently with my shoulder and shook my head at her. I leaned in to whisper in her ear, "The most important thing right now is to find Daisy. Getting into an argument with Lestrade isn't going to help any of us. Move on. Be the bigger person."

Shelby studied me for a few moments, debating on which road she would take. I held my breath, waiting for her to spew an insult.

"*I'm* going to do something useful since Daisy isn't going to be found by sitting around." She exited the room, muttering under her breath, "I'm already the better detective."

Did that really work? Was I able to reason with her? It was a dognapping miracle!

Mrs. Lacy ordered Tamra to follow Shelby while she went to get a refill on Lestrade's coffee.

That left me alone with the detective. I sat down quietly on one of the armchairs in the room, hoping not to draw any attention to myself. The last thing I needed was any problems with the police.

"Weren't you with Holmes the other day at the deli?" Lestrade broke the silence. "What's your name, kid?"

"Ah," I stuttered, as I'd never had to deal with a police

officer before. Sure, there were plenty of security guards and military personnel on the posts, but I was never associated with somebody like Shelby. "I'm John Watson, ma'am. My mother was in the army, and we just moved to New York City. Shelby's my neighbor."

I don't know why I felt the need to share so much, but maybe if she knew that my mom was in the military, she'd know that I wasn't up to any trouble (despite Shelby's intentions).

"Listen, John Watson, let me give you some advice from your friendly neighborhood New York City Police Department: no good can come from hanging out with that girl."

Yeah, I had the feeling.

But . . . And that was the thing with Shelby. As rude and peculiar as she was, it was fun hanging out with her. She was becoming a friend and someone I was learning a lot from (again, *not* as an assistant).

"Yes, ma'am," I replied, because there wasn't any other answer I could've given. The chances were slim that I'd ever cross paths with Detective Lestrade again.

"AHA!" Shelby's voice carried into the living room.

"Great," Lestrade said sarcastically.

We both got up and went into the hallway. Shelby walked out of the dogs' room with a triumphant smile. "Well, look at this. It appears that *I've* found yet another significant clue."

~ CHAPTER ~
19

EVERYBODY RUSHED INTO THE DOG ROOM TO FIND ...
everything looking pretty much the same as it had yesterday.

"What are we looking for?" I asked, eager to see the
latest clue.

Shelby pointed up to the shelf where the dog food was
stored. "That!"

The two containers seemed to be in the same place. But
I also only *saw* them yesterday; I hadn't really *observed*.

Shelby reached up on her tiptoes and pulled down the
container of Daisy's dog food. She held it up and we all
leaned in, trying to decipher whatever clue was in the food.

"Watson." Shelby turned the container to the side and
urged me to look closer.

That was when I saw it. It wasn't something that was easy
to spot. On the side there was a tiny piece of tape stuck to
the container.

So I found the clue, but what did it *mean*?

I pointed at the tape but decided it was best not to even try to make an uneducated guess.

"Yes, you know who put it there?"

The room continued to stare at Shelby. She certainly enjoyed dragging things out. It must be nice to always be the smartest person in the room.

"I did." She set the container down. "I put it at the level of where the food was yesterday at 4:23 p.m."

My head began spinning as I realized what this meant.

"Watson," Shelby prodded me.

"The tape is nearly an inch above the food now," I exclaimed excitedly.

See, I could be more than just an assistant. Maybe I really did have it in me to be a detective. It was such a rush figuring out the clue. Granted, I needed Shelby's help to know where to look and what to look for, but I was still new to this sleuthing stuff.

"I don't get it," Zareen stated.

"It means . . ." Shelby gestured at me.

"It means that somebody took Daisy's dog food after we were in here."

Lestrade leaned against the wall, a bored look on her face. "I believe there are two dogs in this household."

"But they eat different food." I pointed to Roxy's container.

"So somebody made a simple mistake."

Zareen raised her hand timidly. "I was the one who fed Roxy last night, and I can guarantee you that I took the food from her container. We're very strict about their diets."

"I'm sorry." Mrs. Lacy pinched the bridge of her nose. "Can you please explain what this means? Why would somebody take Daisy's dog food? She's not here."

"Exactly!" Shelby's face lit up. "First, this means that Daisy is safe because whoever took her is feeding her. But the biggest clue is this: whoever took her was in this very room at some point after 4:23 yesterday afternoon."

Everybody in the room looked around at each other accusingly.

Now we were really getting somewhere.

CHAPTER 20

"THEN WHO TOOK MY DOG?" TAMRA CRIED OUT as her mom comforted her.

Zareen remained silent, her eyes glued to the food container.

"What's going on?" The trainer walked into the dogs' room. "Why is everybody staring at the food? How is that going to help find Daisy?"

"Could you then enlighten us with what *will* help us find Daisy?" Shelby asked in an innocent tone, although it was clear she was hoping he'd slip up and tell us what he did with her.

If he'd taken her.

Or was it Zareen?

"I've been—" Emerson began until he caught sight of Lestrade's badge. "You called the police? Was that really necessary?"

Hmm. Emerson appeared to be more upset than Shelby

about Lestrade's company. Maybe that was because he was the one who took Daisy! He was here yesterday afternoon! It was him!

I stared at Shelby, waiting for her to arrest him or whatever it was that she did when she captured her perp.

Captured her perp? Great, I was even starting to sound like her.

"We needed to do something," Mrs. Lacy explained. "Detective Lestrade is a friend of the family and offered her assistance."

"To sit and do nothing," Shelby said under her breath, but I nudged her. She needed to stop wasting her energy on Lestrade and start figuring out how the trainer (or Zareen) did it.

"Yes." Lestrade nodded at Emerson. "Well, I'm going to reach out again to the shelters and see if Daisy has shown up. Please call me if you discover any real evidence."

Unbelievable. She walked right by Emerson. Completely clueless that he was one of our main suspects.

Now it was only up to Shelby to figure out what happened. Fast.

Emerson gestured for us to follow him into the living room. "So I went to several pet stores in the neighborhood to deliver some flyers."

Shelby perked up. "Really? Did you find anything out?"

Emerson did a double take at Shelby and took a step back. Probably not wanting to get mowed over again like yesterday. "Everybody was upset to hear what happened. Daisy is a celebrity to dog groomers. Although if Daisy had her collar, someone—"

Shelby cut him off. "Would've called, yes. We're aware of that."

Why wasn't Shelby asking the most pressing question: *Did he do it?* I was tired of discovering clues but not really getting anywhere. I wish she'd just sit them both down and question them until they broke. Something, *anything* to move us forward.

Zareen gasped suddenly. "I'm so sorry, John!" she exclaimed. "With everything going on, I forgot to tell you that Zane is at the park. He said that if you wanted to join him and his friends, you could meet them there. I can show you where they are on a map."

"Oh, thanks." I felt torn. While I was thrilled to get an invitation, I didn't want to abandon Shelby. "But I should stay here and help."

"It's okay," Shelby said. "You should go play with your friends."

"I don't—"

"Really, it's fine, Watson. Go have fun."

I was a little disappointed by her reaction. It seemed like

she wanted me to get out of there (and her way). I thought I was being helpful, but maybe I wouldn't even make a good assistant, let alone a detective.

I turned to follow Zareen to another room, but Shelby stopped me in the hallway. "Before you leave, I would appreciate if you assisted me with a somewhat urgent matter regarding our trainer friend." Her voice was low. "Shouldn't take too long."

I nodded. "I'll be right back."

This was it! This was the moment when she was going to finally make the trainer confess what he'd done. We were getting close! That was why it was okay for me to leave. The case was on the verge of being solved!

Zareen took a map of Central Park out of a drawer. I thought it looked big from the street, but seeing how much of Manhattan the park took up made me a little intimidated to venture into it by myself.

"It's fairly easy to find the courts at the Great Lawn," Zareen explained as she drew a path for me. Maybe for her, but all I could see were the other routes I could take instead that would leave me completely lost.

"Uh, thanks, this is really helpful."

She gave me a forced smile. "You're welcome. I hope you have fun." She pressed her lips together, like she was holding back a sob.

"Are you okay?" I patted her back.

"No." A tear started snaking its way down her cheek. "I know that everybody thinks I did it. But I didn't. I love Daisy. Sure, it's hard always being second-best to your little sister. Even my dog can't compete with hers. But why would I do this? How could I have done it? You probably don't believe me, but I've been home this entire time, except to walk Roxy. I couldn't have taken Daisy."

A wave of guilt overcame me. I'd thought Zareen was guilty almost immediately. While the trainer was starting to look more and more like our culprit, I still had Zareen in my mind as not entirely innocent. Seeing how torn up she was made me realize that there was no way she could've done it. She was too upset to be guilty.

"You want my opinion? I think Tamra did it." She looked like she believed every word she was saying. "She always wants attention. And she usually gets it. Dad promised to take me to Paris for my birthday. But she's always wanted to go. I know if Tamra throws the whole woe-is-me routine about Daisy being 'missing,' he'll cave and agree to take her, too. I overheard her last night crying to him. He asked her what would make her feel better, and she replied 'nothing.' Then he said, 'Well, how about I take you to Paris with us?'"

"What did Tamra say?"

"I don't know. I walked away." Zareen clenched her jaw. "I've always had to share my birthday with Zane. Now I have to share my present with Tamra."

I used to envy the kids at the post who had siblings. Every time they moved, they automatically had someone to rely on. Sure, I had Mom and Dad. Then, when Dad left, all I had was Mom. It would've been nice to have a sibling as well. But after witnessing Zareen's misery, I was wondering if maybe that wasn't the case. Maybe it was better to be on your own.

"I'm so sorry, Zareen," I said, trying to comfort her. "I can't even begin to understand how difficult this has been for you. Listen, Shelby can be a bit rude, but she knows what she's doing. She'll find out who did this and will clear your name."

"You really believe in her?" Zareen asked.

"Yes." I knew Shelby wasn't going to rest until Daisy was found.

"Thanks, John." Zareen wiped away her tears. "I shouldn't tell you all of our family drama, but I really appreciate you listening. I'm rarely heard around here."

I gave her shoulder a little squeeze before I headed back to the living room with my map in hand.

"I'm curious about what you do." Shelby was in the middle of talking with the trainer. Mrs. Lacy and Tamra were looking at the online message board they'd put up about Daisy to see if anybody had seen her. "I have an English bulldog who is an extraordinary animal, and you're one of the best trainers, obviously."

Shelby was slathering on the charm.

Her voice began to rise. "I'd love to pick your brain, if you don't mind?"

"Sure," Emerson replied cautiously. "What would you like to know?"

"Well"—Shelby dropped down to her knees and then knocked over a chair—"oh, I'm so sorry. You know what?" At this point her voice was practically a yell. "Am I disturbing you, Mrs. Lacy? Is there somewhere I could talk to Mr. Emerson in private?"

Emerson looked like a deer caught in headlights. I doubt many people would want to be stuck in a room alone with Shelby.

If he only knew what her real motive was.

Mrs. Lacy glanced up from the computer screen. "Yes, you can use the dining room," she replied, distracted. "We'll be here if you need anything."

"Wonderful!" Shelby stared at Emerson until he finally relented and got up. I followed them into the large dining room with a table that seated twelve.

"Shut the door behind you, Watson."

I obliged.

Then a big smile spread on Shelby's face.

"Watson, please lock the door."

CHAPTER 21

THIS WAS IT.

I knew Shelby had figured it out and was going to make Emerson confess. She'd find Daisy, and the Lacys would get to be a family again.

And I couldn't wait to watch it all unfold (and just in time for me to catch a game with Zane).

"What can I do to help?" Emerson sat down at the head of the long table. Either he was a really good actor or he was oblivious of what Shelby had up her sleeve.

Shelby pulled up a chair right next to him, preparing for her interrogation. "First, can you explain to me why you lied to the Lacys about where you were the last few days?"

Emerson furrowed his eyebrows. "I don't know what you're talking about. I was tending to a very sick aunt. How dare you—"

"You were on an American Airlines flight en route to LaGuardia Airport when the Lacys were trying to get ahold of you. You missed your connection in Dallas because your flight from Cozumel was delayed due to weather. That's why you didn't pick up your cell phone. You had planned to be back by morning, and they would've been none the wiser."

The color drained from Emerson's face, save for his still-sunburned nose. "I wasn't . . ." His lips kept moving, but it appeared that he had lost his voice (or his nerve—probably both).

"Let's skip the charade where you pretend that I'm wrong and get down to business: who took Daisy?"

"Wait!" I cried out. "You mean he didn't do it?"

Shelby looked disappointed in me. "Of course not, Watson. He was on a plane when the crime occurred. That's about as solid an alibi as they come. But that doesn't mean he didn't have an accomplice."

No! I was positive the trainer did it.

But the only other real lead we had was Zareen, and she didn't do it.

I let out a little moan before slumping over the chair nearest to Shelby.

"It's his first case," Shelby explained to a confused Emerson.

"Listen," Emerson said slowly, as if he knew that every word out of his mouth could be used against him. "I had nothing to do with the disappearance of Daisy. I adore that dog. I've been running myself ragged posting flyers and talking to anybody who could help."

"Which is exactly what a guilty person would do," Shelby replied. "Now, let me ask you again. Why did you lie to the Lacys about where you were?"

Emerson looked at the door, probably planning an escape. He then leaned forward and placed his head in his hands. "They would've been upset at me for leaving so close to a show, even though I knew I'd be back in plenty of time. It was sort of a last-minute vacation. I got a deal online for this trip—as you can imagine, I don't make a ton of money. I wanted to do something nice for my new girlfriend."

"So wouldn't rigging the competition get you a ton of money?" Shelby fired back.

"What?" His face was scrunched up, and I kind of felt bad for the guy. Here he was, working for a very wealthy family, and the only way he could afford a vacation was to scour the Internet for deals. It must've been hard to keep up with the Lacys. "I'd never hurt Daisy, or any dog. I love what I do. It doesn't give me a lot of free time, but I would never—and I mean *never*—do anything to Daisy."

"You have all the elements of someone who is guilty: motive, keys to the apartment—you were in the apartment yesterday and could've taken the food. Am I correct?" Shelby asked, but I was fairly certain that was a rhetorical question because everybody in the room already knew she was right.

"I have keys because I walk the dogs during the day when the girls are at school. No one would—" It was as if a light had turned on over his head.

"What?" Shelby leaned forward so she was only inches away from him. "What are you thinking? You know something!"

He shook his head. "It's probably nothing."

"Let me be the judge of that."

"Well, the only other people who have access to the apartment are the staff and the family."

"Correct."

"Right before I left, I was working with Roxy. That dog has been really challenging—I've never experienced such a stubborn animal. It's amazing such a tiny dog can make so much noise." (So far his story checked out.) "Zareen came up to me and said she wanted to start entering her in competitions. I advised her against it. At this stage, Roxy isn't ready. One bark at a judge and it's over."

"And?" Shelby prodded him, getting as impatient as I was to find out what he knew.

"Now, listen, Zareen's a good girl, but she's going through a rough time. She got upset and stormed out of the room, but the last thing she said to me was, 'I wish someone would take me away from this family, or at least get rid of that goody-two-shoes dog.'"

"No!" I gasped. "There's no way Zareen did it. She told me earlier and, well, I believed her."

I did. Didn't I?

Shelby turned her attention back to Emerson. "How peculiar that this is the first time you're bringing this up."

"I was too preoccupied with my vacation, and I didn't really think of it at the time. Zareen is prone to outbursts, so I simply chalked it up to that. Then, when I returned, I was so focused on finding Daisy it didn't even occur to me until now."

A rattling came from the dining room door. "Why is the door locked?" Tamra asked on the other side as she began pounding on it. "Shelby! Open up!"

Shelby strode over to the door and opened it.

On the other side, Tamra held up a piece of clear glass. "We have another clue!"

CHAPTER
22

SHELBY GRABBED THE PIECE OF GLASS WITHOUT ANY CAUTION. "Is this what I think it is?"

"Yes—it's part of the picture frame that's missing!" Tamra replied excitedly.

As much as Emerson wanted to point fingers at Zareen, maybe Zareen had a point: Tamra certainly was getting a lot of attention from this. Her demeanor had gone from mourning and worried to giddy.

But would she bring us a clue if she was the one to hide Daisy? Didn't she say that Daisy hardly ever barked? Maybe, just maybe, Daisy was still in the house! Yes! Tamra was the one who smuggled Daisy's dog food. She was setting Zareen up. It was all making sense to me.

I needed to get Shelby away from everybody so I could share my theory with her, but she jogged off with Tamra upstairs. I followed to find a woman dressed in an actual maid's uniform (I thought that was only in the movies!) dusting the bureau.

"Karina," Tamra addressed the maid, "please show us exactly where you found this."

The maid nodded, unaware of the excitement that finding a piece of glass had caused. "I was going to vacuum the rugs. When I bent down to plug in the vacuum, I saw the glass under the bureau. I picked it up, didn't think anything of it, and that's when you came along, Miss Tamra."

How *convenient* for Tamra to appear right when the piece of evidence, which she had to have planted, was discovered. If memory served, I believed it was Tamra who realized that the frame was missing in the first place. She also basically accused Zareen of knocking it over because she sleepwalks.

It was all coming together.

At this point, I could only hope that Shelby wouldn't fall for it.

Shelby knelt down and looked behind the bureau. "I can't believe I didn't see it yesterday." She clenched her teeth together. Shelby probably wasn't used to missing anything. But she had.

"Shelby, can I talk to you?" I asked in a low voice, hoping I could tell her that I figured it all out before she swooped in and declared that Zareen had done it.

"What's going on?" Mrs. Lacy came upstairs, with Zareen behind her.

"Look what Karina found!" Tamra handed her mother the glass and gave a quick glance at Zareen.

She was so ready to set her up. I couldn't stand by and let an innocent person be accused of something that they didn't do. This wasn't fair! Zareen had been through enough.

"Shelby . . ." I tried to get Shelby's attention as she was busy measuring the length of the bureau. Then she bent down to measure the small sliver of hardwood floor between the rug and the wall.

"What is it, Watson?" Shelby took a step back and looked at the bureau with her head tilted in one direction and then the other. She then took a few paces from Zareen's room to the bureau.

No, no, no . . . She needed to know there was a conspiracy afoot!

"Can I talk to you?"

"Yes." Shelby closed her eyes and walked into the bureau.

Zareen studied Shelby's actions with tears welling up in her eyes. She knew what was coming.

If only I could get Shelby alone.

"Oh, this?" Mrs. Lacy attention finally went from Shelby to the glass that was placed in her hand. "You know it wasn't expensive. It's only a frame."

"But!" Tamra said excitedly. "It was broken during the night that Daisy went missing. We all know that Zareen sleepwalks, so she must've broken it!"

"It wouldn't be the first time Zareen has broken something, honey." Mrs. Lacy gave her older daughter a warm smile, but Zareen returned it with a grimace. "It's just a broken picture frame. It doesn't really mean anything."

"Actually, it does," Shelby interrupted. "How would a frame break when there is carpet on all sides of the bureau, except for the back? It would've had to have been a precise hit to this small opening, and there's only one angle that would work."

"Shelby," I warned her. "I really need to talk to you."

"In a minute," she said, dismissing me.

All eyes were on Shelby. She went to the entryway of Zareen's bedroom and began to shuffle her feet as she walked forward. Her foot hit the thin runner that ran along the majority of the hallway. She then slowly pretended to fall. Her body moved in a deliberate, almost graceful manner as her shoulder hit the corner of the bureau where the broken frame would've been the night of the crime.

"This is what happened to the frame," she declared as I stared her down, willing her to stop talking. "Zareen was sleepwalking; her foot caught on the rug, which propelled her body forward. As she is six and three-eighths inches

169

taller than me, her arm would've knocked over the frame, which would've hit the wall"—Shelby took masking tape out of her bag, tore off a piece, and stuck it on the wall—"right here!" She rubbed the tape a few times before pulling the piece away.

She held up the tape for us to see that there were tiny particles of glass, nearly invisible to the naked eye, on the tape.

"I don't remember breaking it—I swear!" Zareen protested. I stood beside her and placed my hand on her shoulder.

Somebody needed to be on her side. She certainly wasn't getting any support from her family or Shelby. In fact, if she had taken Daisy, I wouldn't have really blamed her.

"That's not the point I'm making," Shelby replied. She turned to the maid. "So you didn't clean up the broken frame prior to the discovery of this missing piece?"

"No." She shook her head. "This was the first time I saw anything. Whenever I discover anything broken, I always report it to Mrs. Lacy."

"What does this mean?" Tamra asked, practically begging Shelby to accuse Zareen right here and now.

"It means that yes, Zareen broke the picture frame the night Daisy disappeared, but that doesn't necessarily mean she cleaned it up."

Zareen relaxed slightly upon hearing this.

"It also doesn't mean she didn't."

Her shoulders skyrocketed back to her ears.

I couldn't take it anymore. "*Or* it was someone who was trying to set Zareen up and left the frame piece as evidence against her!"

Zareen gave me a grateful smile through her tears, while Tamra began to protest. It appeared that Tamra was all too eager to lay the blame on somebody else.

"What this does mean," Shelby said with a raise of her eyebrow, "is that the person who cleaned up the broken picture frame was the person who took Daisy."

"I'm not sure I understand," Mrs. Lacy said with a sigh, becoming unnerved from all the clues that *hadn't* led us to the person who took Daisy.

"What happens when you wake up to discover that Zareen has broken something in her sleep?"

"We clean it up," she stated before stealing a glance at Karina. "Well, Karina cleans it up. And we make sure Zareen's okay, of course."

Interesting that the safety of her daughter was her second thought. Maybe Mrs. Lacy did it! Maybe she was the one framing Zareen!

I mean, someone had to have done it. At this point, I was willing to throw out any possibilities as long as it wasn't Zareen.

"So you'd be aware that something had happened. Having broken glass in the hallway would've certainly tipped you off to the fact that Zareen, or somebody else, was wandering around the house late at night. So whoever cleaned it up either didn't want you to know she did it—"

"But I didn't!" Zareen howled. "Even though I never remember sleepwalking, the bell always wakes somebody up! I couldn't have done it!"

Shelby held up her hand to silence Zareen. "I believe I have successfully proved that you did sleepwalk that night and did indeed break the frame. But as I was saying, it was either Zareen *or* someone who didn't want attention brought to the fact that Zareen was sleepwalking, so they cleaned up the mess."

"So she was set up!" I nearly screamed. It was about time that Shelby realized that she was barking up the wrong tree. *Ugh.* Now *I* was starting to make bad dog puns.

"No, Watson. Whoever did this *didn't* want Zareen to be accused or they would've left the entire shattered frame for us to point the finger at her."

Tamra quickly did just that and pointed her finger accusingly at her sister. "She did it. She was covering her tracks!"

Zareen's entire body was shaking as she lost her battle against a tidal wave of tears. "You believe me, Watson?" she asked between sobs.

"I do," I replied. I turned to Shelby. "I really do, Shelby. She didn't do it."

Shelby replied with a roll of her eyes, a reaction I was getting used to.

"Listen, sweetie," Mrs. Lacy said to Tamra. "I think we have to call the dog show organizers to let them know that you aren't showing Daisy tomorrow."

Tamra began to protest, but Shelby cut her off. "Don't do that. I have a theory that I need to test out by watching the security footage."

"Which is?" Mrs. Lacy prodded her.

"I'd rather wait for all the evidence to come forward before I give my verdict, but, Tamra, trust me. You will be showing Daisy tomorrow. You have my word."

"Your *word*? I'd rather have my *dog*," she said, sulking. She then grabbed her sister's arm. "This whole thing would be a lot easier if you just confessed to what you did to my dog!"

"I. DIDN'T. TAKE. HER," Zareen screamed before marching into her room and slamming the door.

Great. We were now back to the Lacys fighting.

"Shelby," Mrs. Lacy said, her voice hoarse, "I don't want to seem like I don't believe you, but this is tearing my family apart. How confident are you that you can locate Daisy soon? I don't care about the competition tomorrow. I care about my family."

"I promise. A detective is only as good as her reputation, and if you ask around, you'll find that mine is flawless."

Mrs. Lacy didn't seem too convinced. "Well, I certainly hope so." She started to rap lightly on Zareen's door.

Shelby began walking down the stairs. "Where are you going?" I called after her.

"I've got security footage to watch. Don't you have a game of the basketball to play?"

"It's just 'basketball,'" I corrected her, although it cracked me up that she referred to it as "*the* basketball." Man, she really knew nothing about sports.

"Yes, but you seem to be eager to play." (My grammar lesson apparently went over her head.)

I had been looking forward to playing ever since I saw Zane with a ball in his hands when we first met. This was my chance.

"Are you sure you don't need my help watching footage?" I offered.

"I think I can manage more than adequately on my own."

"Listen, Shelby." I looked around to make sure nobody could hear us. "I know that Zareen didn't do it. Tamra is setting her up. Or maybe Mrs. Lacy? Or the trainer? All I know is that Zareen didn't do it."

"Is there a member of this family you don't have a crush on?" She snorted.

"Shelby . . ."

"You want to know why it's not a good idea to make friends, especially ones involved in a case?" she asked with her arms folded. "Because it can cloud your vision. I don't let feelings and emotions influence me. The facts will speak for themselves. That's the only thing I'm interested in. Having friends only complicates matters."

I stood there with my mouth open. I felt like I was making some headway with Shelby, that she was beginning to trust me. That she and I were becoming friends. But how wrong I was. I never felt so stupid around Shelby as I did then, and that was saying something.

Shelby ignored me as she dug her hand in her backpack, while anger grew inside me.

She only thought of me as a burden. It was clear she wanted me to leave so I could get out of her hair. I was only useful to her if I was locking a door or walking her dog.

"You know what?" I snapped. "I care about others. People are humans with emotions, not merely pawns in your investigation. Maybe you'd get further in your cases or, I don't know, with people your own age if you didn't treat them with such spite. It's like you don't care about anybody or anything, except your cases."

Shelby looked at me blankly. It was then that I realized she was holding out something in her hands. It was a bottle of water, an orange, and a string cheese wrapped in plastic.

"What's that?" I asked, confused why she wasn't mad at my outburst. Why she wasn't fighting back. She always had a quick reply ready.

"I brought you a snack to ensure that you had proper energy before you played with the basketball. Shouldn't you have an afternoon snack?"

With everything going on with the case, she was concerned about my diabetes?

"Oh, thanks." I took her offering meekly, ashamed of my outburst.

Hold on. How did she know that I was even going to play basketball this afternoon? This *was* her plan all along: dump me off on Zane. All Shelby wanted was to find Daisy, not make friends, especially with me.

But then why would she bring me a snack? Maybe she did care?

Apparently, Daisy's disappearance wasn't the only mystery around here.

"Well?" Shelby opened the door and gestured for me to leave the apartment with her. "Ready?"

I didn't know what to say. How to feel about everything she had said. It wasn't like I could take a nutritional snack as an offering of friendship.

Shelby didn't have friends. She didn't need friends.

But I did.

And there was only one way I was going to get them.

"Ready."

CHAPTER 23

As I took a few steps out from the Lacys' building into the sunny day, I realized this was really my first time out in the city alone.

I was free!

Yet there was something that kept pulling me back to the building.

Guilt flooded me for leaving Zareen with people who were convinced that she stole her own sister's dog.

I looked at the already-half-eaten snack Shelby had given me.

Maybe I also felt bad for leaving Shelby. Although how many ways could one person let you know you weren't wanted?

This was always my problem. Even back on the post, I always felt bad for the one kid sitting by himself at lunch. Mom used to praise me for looking out for others. "The little guardian," she used to call me when I'd bring the latest stray home.

Sure, I had a bunch of friends and probably could've been considered popular or whatever. But I always had a soft spot when someone needed help. I could never turn my back on anybody.

I guess when you'd lived in so many places, you knew what it felt like to be the new kid. I was that kid practically every other year. So there's that army-post mentality that we're all in this together. Sometimes there was such a small community you pretty much didn't have much of a choice.

But this was New York City. I could do anything and be friends with anybody.

Maybe that was what was terrifying about it. Before, if I made a bad choice about who I sat with at lunch or got on the bad side of a teacher, it really didn't matter, as I wasn't going to be sticking around for that long. There weren't real consequences.

Now everything seemed like a big deal. Maybe because this city was huge. The fact was that in a few weeks I'd be at a school where the only people I knew were Shelby, a genius with questionable social skills, and Tamra, a girl who might possibly be setting her sister up for a crime she didn't commit.

As I crossed Central Park West, leaving the tall, brick residences that loomed over the park's outskirts, I could see the signs up for Daisy.

Trust your gut, John.

That was what my dad used to tell me all the time.

That was why I'd always sit down with the person who was alone, knowing how it would feel if that were me. That might be me at the Academy.

My gut at that moment was screaming to me that Zareen was innocent. It told me that she was being set up.

But my gut had been wrong before.

It had told me that Shelby needed a friend, when it seemed like she couldn't get rid of me fast enough.

It had told me that moving to New York City would make everything easier, when, in fact, it made everything harder. While I was used to new places, this was a whole new life.

My gut had also told me that things were going to be okay. That Dad was going to stay. But it was wrong.

Maybe I shouldn't ever trust my gut after all.

I'd been so lost in my thoughts that I suddenly realized I had no idea where I was. I looked down at the map. Everywhere around me, there were trees and grass, people riding bikes and lying on blankets, soaking in the sun. I spun in a circle trying to see if I could spot the two towers of the Lacys' building to get my bearings. Even though I was in the middle of this huge city, it felt like a regular park. Well, a giant, huge park that was easy to get lost in. You'd think I'd be able to find something called the Great Lawn.

Yeah, you'd think.

You'd also think a kid could believe his own father.

I turned around, trying to get a sense of north and south. All I wanted to do was start my new life with some new friends, but instead I was turning around like a dog trying to catch its tail.

"Excuse me?" I asked a couple walking by. They replied in some foreign language. I tried to stop a few others, but if they didn't have their headphones on or were distracted by their phones, they assumed I was trying to sell them something. Up ahead, I saw some kids walking in a group, one of them was dribbling a ball.

I sped up to follow them. Maybe they were going to the same court. Or they'd at least be helpful.

I was eager to start playing some ball. Not only because it would be with some new people, but it also reminded me of my time with Dad. We'd usually shoot some hoops on the weekend or if he got home from work early. It was a pretty simple thing, but every time I held a ball in my hands, it would remind me of him. And since he was currently hundreds of miles away and not taking Mom's calls, memories were all I had.

Was that how things were going to be now? Whenever I left a post, I had all these friends and we always promised to stay in touch. Sure, there'd be a few messages in the first couple of months, but then they'd stop. I'd made new friends, and they'd moved on. It was like that saying: Out of sight, out of mind.

But he wasn't a friend; he was my dad.

I shook my head to get back to focusing on the game and making some friends. After a couple more minutes, I finally arrived at the basketball courts. I started scanning the different games. There were so many people it took me a second to find Zane, but relief overcame me as I spotted him and his friends in a corner court.

Maybe things weren't going to be bad here after all.

Sure, I didn't know what was going on with Dad. I also had no clue what Shelby's deal was: one minute she treated me like a friend, the other she was dismissive of me. But now I could forget all that and have an afternoon of playing ball with some guys.

I waved at Zane as I jogged toward him.

"There he is!" Zane called out to me as I tried to silence the butterflies in my stomach.

It's only a game, I told myself. *It's only meeting the people who could become your close friends.*

Yeah, no pressure.

"Yo!" Zane called out to his friends, who paused their game. "You got to meet my new friend."

My head swirled with pride at the word *friend*.

The group of eight guys gathered in the center of their court while I was introduced around. Luckily, when you make new friends every couple years, you become used to memorizing names pretty quickly. I made sure to say each person's name to try to get it stuck in my head. I decided to start filling my brain attic with a whole container filled with "new friends."

"What's up? I'm Corey." A tall guy who seemed much older than the rest of the group held out his fist, and unlike Shelby, I knew to return the bump.

"Hey, Corey, I'm Watson," I replied, surprised that Shelby's new nickname came out of my mouth. I had to admit, I was getting used to it. Plus, it was better than being just another John.

"Cool." Corey nodded at me.

You know what? It *was* pretty cool.

Another with a huge Afro lifted his chin at me. "Hey, man, I'm Jake, this is Antonio," he said as he threw the ball to a guy in a Brooklyn Nets jersey.

"Let's see what you can do," Antonio said as he passed the ball to me.

I had to remind myself that it had only been a week since I last played with my buddies in Maryland. It had seemed so much longer than that.

I found my rhythm pretty quickly. Did a few dribbles, then faked Corey out by pretending to go to my left, but went to my right instead and sank the ball into the basket.

"Nice shot, John!" Zane called out as we went on defense.

I was able to steal the ball away and pass it to Zane, who went in for an easy layup, but missed, much to the delight of the opposing team.

"Dude!" Antonio called out with a laugh. "That's what you get for bailing on us. You get rusty!"

"Please," Zane retorted. "I figure you guys need a break every once in a while so you get a chance to score."

"Yeah." Corey bumped into Antonio. "You're just jealous Zane bought me these sick kicks. The sweeter the shoes, the sweeter our victory."

They all groaned before continuing to play.

Just like that, everything felt natural, easy. This was where I belonged. With people who didn't overanalyze me the second they met me. Who simply wanted to spend the afternoon playing ball and hanging. They didn't make me feel stupid or useless.

We were equals. We could be friends.

No accusations. No drama.

Shelby's voice from earlier today came into my head unexpectedly: *Observe. Remember everything.*

I did want to remember everything about this afternoon, not because I had to report back to Shelby on her assignment but because it was fun. The other morning, sitting on that stoop, I felt so lost and overwhelmed, wondering how I was going to be able to make friends in this insanely large and intimidating place.

Here I was, a little over forty-eight hours later, playing with a new group of potential friends.

See, I didn't need Shelby. I was doing fine on my own.

Despite almost getting lost, I made it here.

Corey blocked one of my shots, which knocked me down to the ground.

"Sorry, Watson." He held out his hand to help me up.

"No problem."

These guys weren't so different from my old friends.

There was the requisite teasing that took place during any games between friends. We took a few breaks to hydrate. They all had those expensive (and sugary) sports drinks that I'd always seen on TV, while I drank the water that Shelby had given me. I was even more grateful for it now. Back on the post, we'd just run home if we were thirsty or hungry since the court was usually only a couple blocks away from home. It hadn't even occurred to me to bring anything.

"So where you from?" Antonio asked.

"All over," I began to explain. "I'm what you would call an army brat, most recently from Maryland, but before that, Kentucky, Georgia, and Texas."

"Sweet!" Corey replied. "I've lived here my whole life, but I'm finally breaking free in a couple weeks to go to school at Rutgers. Even though it's only in New Jersey."

I didn't realize we were playing with a college kid. I felt even better about my basketball skills since I was able to score a couple points on him.

Corey continued, "Must be cool to see so much of the country."

The others nodded, like spending your entire life in New York City was boring.

I was sure you could become accustomed to wherever you live, but I couldn't ever imagine having a dismissive attitude to living here.

"What's it like living on a military base?" Jake asked.

"It's called a post," I corrected him, but then I felt like Shelby for doing it. So what if he wanted to call it a base? "It's pretty awesome." I might have slightly exaggerated. I mean, I liked having a little community of friends who knew what it was like to move all over the place. Or to have a family member serving overseas. But this was New York City, and it was awesome from whatever angle you looked at it.

"You've ever been in a tank?" Antonio asked. "Or a fighter jet?"

I did my best to not laugh at their questions. It was kind of nice to be someone who was different in a good way. I was the new kid. I was a breath of fresh air for them.

"Did your dad go abroad?" Zane asked.

"No, my mom did. She was in Afghanistan."

"Whoa." Zane nodded in awe. "Your mom must be pretty tough."

"Yeah, she is."

Zane hit Jake. "I wonder if she's as tough as Candace."

The group began laughing and started talking about people and inside jokes, which left me a little clueless. Luckily, I was able to rejoin the conversation once they moved on to a discussion of the chances we all thought the Yankees had to make the play-offs.

"As long as your bullpen stays healthy, you've got a real shot," I remarked.

"Yes!" Corey slapped me on the back. "Watson here knows what he's talking about. It all comes down to the pitchers."

I nodded like I've been following the Yankees for years. Although this was something I always did before I went to a new place—become an expert on the local sports team. When in doubt (and out of things to talk about with new guy friends), go with sports. So the last two weeks, I'd brushed up on all professional New York City teams—and it was work since there are so many of them: two baseball teams, two basketball teams, two football teams, and two hockey teams.

It was the most homework I'd ever had to do before moving.

After seeing the Yankees and Knicks posters on Zane's walls yesterday, I narrowed down my research and did some light reading last night on the Yankees' current season.

Truthfully, I could've stayed there all day. It was only when Zane looked at his phone that I realized it was getting late in the afternoon. I'd promised Mom that I'd be home for dinner and I didn't want to completely ignore her for my new friends. I knew she'd understand, but she was new to this city, too. We were both starting over.

"I gotta bounce," Zane announced to the group. He took his blue-and-orange messenger bag and slung it over his shoulder.

The other guys began to disperse, all telling me they'd catch me later.

I wanted to ask when or get their information but didn't want to appear desperate. I began to follow Zane out of the courts, not wanting to get lost again.

"What was the house like when you were there?" Zane asked, his voice laced with worry.

"I'm not going to lie. It was a little intense." I wondered if Zareen and Tamra always fought like that. "I feel bad for Zareen. I think she's going to be blamed for it."

He sighed. "Ugh. That's what I was afraid of. You have to understand, Zareen's my twin. I've always been protective of her. I can tell you she didn't do it. There's no way."

"Did you hear the bell ring the other night when she was sleepwalking?" I asked, because even though he and I were simply hanging, I couldn't get the case out of my head.

"Naw, she wasn't sleepwalking." He shoved his hands in his pockets. "I would've heard her."

"Well." I debated telling him what Shelby found out, but I knew he was going to eventually hear about it. "Shelby proved that she was sleepwalking that night."

Zane's head jerked to look at me. "How? You know what,

189

it doesn't matter. Even if she was sleepwalking, it doesn't mean that Zareen took Daisy. Whenever we find a bug at our place in the Hamptons, she always puts it outside. She's the kindest person. She didn't do it."

"I know," I replied, because I believed her. I was tempted to ask him what he thought of my theory that Tamra was setting her up, but I didn't want to offend him. Tamra was still his little sister.

"Daisy is a cute dog and all, but there's been nothing but tension since Tamra started putting her in dog shows. Honestly, I thought that if Daisy missed a show, maybe things could get back to normal at our house. But I guess not."

"Yeah." I was struggling for something to say, but then I decided to go for broke. "So who do *you* think did it?"

He shrugged. "I don't know. I think we're overreacting—I mean, Daisy's a good dog. Whoever took her will bring her back. If the person meant her harm, we would've heard by now." He dribbled the ball in his hand for a few seconds. "Who does Shelby think did it?"

"Beats me. She has her theories but isn't sharing," I confessed. "I mean, not like we're close friends or anything—I only met her a couple days ago." I winced at the fact that I felt the need to distance myself from Shelby in front of Zane. Was I going to start becoming one of those guys who made fun of people behind their backs? That wasn't who I was.

Or maybe I was now?

"Dude, I was wondering what the deal was with you two. You're so chill and she's so . . . weird!"

I couldn't help but laugh a little in response, but the second the laugh escaped my throat, I felt guilty. Despite Shelby's knack for being different, she had taken me around the city. She was responsible for the fact that I had Zane and his crew as friends.

We arrived at the outskirts of the park, with Zane's apartment building a few blocks uptown.

"Well, it was awesome hanging with you, John," Zane said as he reached out his fist for me to bump. "We'll do it again soon. Cool?"

"Sure," I said evenly, not trying to show how excited his offer made me.

"Look, I better get back to the drama. Catch you later!" Zane jogged across the street.

It was then I realized I didn't know how to get home. Shelby and I rode the subway here, and I thought I could find it. It was only a couple blocks away, although there was another subway station across the street, but was it the same line? I thought the one we needed was red.

I reached in my pocket for the MetroCard that Shelby

helped me buy so I could pay for my subway trip. I hoped it would have a map or something on it. But it only had the yellow-and-blue MetroCard logo on the front.

Yet another thing Shelby had helped me with. I'd really be lost without her.

Because I was without her and really lost.

I began looking around, wondering if I should go back to the Lacys' to see if Shelby was still there, but I felt that it was as good a time as any to start showing some independence. It was relying on Shelby too much that had led me to this point in the first place.

I could make it on my own. I didn't need her.

A noise from the bushes on the corner startled me. The branches began swaying and I took a step back, afraid of what kind of animal might be lurking there. The only animals I thought the park had outside the zoo were rats and pigeons. I definitely didn't want to see a rat that could make a bush move that much.

Then an annoyed grunt came from the bush as an agitated Shelby stepped out from the branches.

"Watson!" she scolded me as she removed a twig from her hair. "I had hoped you'd eventually move, as I'm attempting to tail a suspect."

"Suspect?" I asked. "Who were you—"

Then I stopped myself. I already knew who it was.

"Shelby"—I tried to keep my voice even—"please tell me you're not following the one guy friend I've made?"

"You may want to rethink the people you choose as acquaintances," she commented before crossing the street.

Tell me about it.

CHAPTER
24

I FOLLOWED SHELBY AS WE KEPT OUR DISTANCE FROM ZANE.

This was silly. He told me he was going home. I tried to explain as much to Shelby, but she ignored me (no surprise there).

We were two blocks away from the apartment building when Zane took a left onto 88th Street.

My throat tensed as we turned the corner, but we stayed on the opposite side of the street at least a half block away so we wouldn't be spotted.

Maybe he is simply running an errand, I tried to explain to the sinking feeling in my stomach. *He didn't say he was going straight home. He is allowed to do other things.*

But Shelby wasn't going to spend her time following someone unless she had a good reason.

"What did you find when you looked at the footage?" I asked cautiously, afraid of the answer.

"A few things, actually," she replied before pulling me

behind a parked truck as Zane was on the corner across from us at a stoplight. "Do you have anything to report from your assignment?"

I was about to ask what assignment until I remembered what she told me before I left, that I was supposed to observe everything. Was that the reason Shelby was eager for me to leave: so I could spy? "You mean besides the fact that we had fun?" I replied defensively.

"Please take this seriously, Watson." Shelby peeked around the truck and then signaled me to continue walking. "Are you sure you didn't hear anything unusual?"

"No, it was just guys playing ball." Although I was positive that Shelby could never fully understand that friends can hang out simply as friends.

"Which means . . ." she prodded me.

"*Which means* we had fun." Even though I knew it was pointless, I began telling her, in the detail she so loved, about the game. I knew she couldn't possibly understand some of the terms, and okay, once I referred to a layup as a "gliding pirouette" just to see if she was as clueless about basketball as she claimed (spoiler alert: she was). But then I got excited about Jake, Corey, and all the other guys I met. I found myself basically telling her everything we talked about.

Shelby remained silent the entire time. Every once in a

while, she'd say "Interesting . . ." but she seemed distracted. Or maybe she wasn't interested at all about my afternoon.

"That was the bag that Zane had?" Shelby interrupted my story about the Yankees play-off discussion as she pointed across the street to Zane's messenger bag.

"Yeah." It seemed pretty clear to me that it was the bag he had since we had come directly from the park.

"I notice that you're wearing tennis shoes. Is that the appropriate footwear that one should wear when playing a game of the basketball?"

She was kidding, right? This was a joke. I took a few moments to reply since I was waiting for her punch line.

Although I didn't think she was capable of making a joke.

"Ah, you wear tennis shoes, sneakers, trainers, whatever you want to call them."

"So you wouldn't wear flip-flops?"

I know she'd said she didn't have any room in her brain attic for sports trivia, but it was like she'd never even seen any sports being played ever, even on TV.

I wanted to tease her for not knowing, but I didn't appreciate it when she was curt to me, so I decided to show her how someone *should* behave when answering a question (albeit a completely ridiculous one). "It would be pretty difficult to play with flip-flops."

"I see," she replied with a nod.

Zane was up ahead, walking past fancy boutiques and restaurants with colorful awnings. We were about forty blocks south of where we lived, but the streets were completely different. The sidewalks were mostly filled with women pushing strollers in workout clothes that looked nicer than what my mom usually wears to work. But inter-mixed with the stores that I was pretty sure I couldn't even afford to walk into were stores from every suburban town I'd ever lived. There was something strangely comforting about seeing a Dunkin' Donuts every few blocks in the middle of a large city.

Zane turned onto Columbus Avenue, and we followed.

It was time for me to finally ask the questions. "Why are you following Zane? What exactly did you find?"

"Do you really want to know?" Shelby asked with a raised eyebrow. Then she grabbed my elbow and led me across the street as Zane disappeared from our view as he turned onto 92nd Street.

"Of course I do!" Although I didn't want to listen to her accuse Zane. There was no way he could've done it. He knew that everybody was blaming Zareen, the person he was closest to. The person he always looked out for. Why would he do something that would only make Zareen miserable?

She sighed impatiently. "I'm merely checking out each family member, so you have nothing to worry about. I know you've become attached to the Lacys, but you do realize that *somebody* had to have taken Daisy. She didn't simply disappear into thin air. All I'm doing is following the facts. And right now those facts have led us here."

We turned the corner onto 92nd Street to discover that Zane was gone. He'd simply vanished.

"Where did he go?" I asked.

Shelby began to walk slowly up the street, cautiously peering into each store window before moving on to the next. Her eyes swept the buildings on the other side of the street until they settled on a store directly across from us.

"There." She pointed at the store. "While always being right can sometimes be a burden, I truly am sorry about this, Watson. Really, I am."

My gaze followed her finger to the bright blue awning with white paw prints.

PAWESOME POOCHES.

CHAPTER
25

THERE WERE MANY, MANY TIMES I'VE BEEN CONFUSED IN THE short while I've known Shelby. Many times. But I had no idea why Shelby was practically gleeful that Zane was in a dog store. His family has dogs. His twin sister has a dog. This wasn't a big deal.

Right?

We remained hidden behind a parked car across the street as we waited. I wasn't exactly sure what we were waiting for.

I couldn't take the silence anymore. "I don't understand why we're hiding. I'm sure there's a perfectly reasonable explanation for Zane going into a dog store."

"Perhaps," she replied cryptically. "Although this gives me an idea. So we will need to go into the store once he leaves."

"Like, to case the joint?"

Case the joint? Really, Watson?

"Something like that."

"Why can't we go in there now?"

"We can't have Zane blow our cover."

While I was excited about going undercover, I was becoming increasingly agitated that Shelby thought Zane was a suspect.

After a few minutes (according to Shelby's stopwatch, it was precisely eight minutes and twelve seconds), Zane emerged from the store. To get a better view, I leaned over the hood of a car, but my balance finally gave way and I fell in front of the car with a thud. "Ow!" I screamed out before I could stop myself.

"Watson?" I heard Zane's voice call out at the same time Shelby cursed me under her breath.

Zane jogged across the street and gave me a hand to help me up. Shelby stayed crouched down. She untied her shoelaces while giving me a glare that made it painfully obvious that she was not happy with me.

"Are you okay?" Zane asked. "What are you guys doing here? Were you hiding?"

"We're here to do some research," Shelby replied quickly. "I was simply tying my shoe while Watson was experimenting with gravity and failed miserably."

"Oh, okay." He looked between us. "Please tell me you'll find Daisy soon. I'm sick that Zareen's being blamed for it. In fact—" Zane reached into his messenger bag and pulled out a Pawesome Pooches' shopping bag. "I figured she needed some cheering up, so I got Roxy this." He held up a stuffed giraffe.

Relief spread through my body. I *knew* there was a simple explanation. Why did Shelby have to make everything a big deal?

"I think it's great you're being so thorough," Zane said to Shelby.

"Thank you," Shelby replied with a hint of sarcasm (so, you know, her regular voice).

"I'll leave you two sleuths to it," he said before heading back the way he came.

"Well, that was a relief," I said, but Shelby's attention was on the store.

She straightened up, pushed her shoulders back, and seemed taller than her usual slumped position. She reached into her backpack and pulled out a pink sequined headband and pushed it on her head to somewhat tame her wild curls.

"Follow my lead," she commanded as we crossed the street and entered the shop.

I'd never been in a pet store before. There hadn't been a need since Dad was allergic to dogs and cats. But I was very certain that even if I'd been to a million pet stores in every single state I'd lived in, nothing would've compared to this.

Sure, there were leashes, bones, and toys, but there was also a section for designer "pet couture," where I picked up a furry jacket, but immediately put it back when I saw it was over seven hundred dollars because it was a mink coat. For a dog.

Let me repeat myself: a mink coat *For a dog.*

There was also a dog perfume counter, a spa for dogs, and a dog bakery.

I should've known the glass case was filled with delicious-looking cookies, biscuits, and cakes that were not for humans, or Shelby would've been over there slobbering just like the black Lab whose paws were currently on the case.

"Can I help you?" An older woman wearing a T-shirt with a fluffy dog on it approached us.

"Yes." Shelby turned around, and I hardly recognized her. I mean, it was definitely Shelby, but she'd also put on a pink cardigan over her baggy black shirt, which was now tucked into her shorts. Her posture was as straight as a pole and her voice seemed to be dripping with honey. She looked like a . . . *girl.* "I'm Petunia Cumberbatch, from the Greenwich Cumberbatches."

Petunia Cumberbatch? Really? And she had made fun of the names *I* had come up with?

"Daddy is waiting outside in his town car—you know how those Wall Street hedge-fund managers are—but I told him I'd pop in and see if this would be an appropriate place for us to store our beloved pooch, Peaches, while we vacation in Saint Bart's. Usually we can take him on our private jet, but it seems that the new chef at our beach house is allergic to dogs, so here we are."

Ah, what?

Shelby had done a complete turnaround of character. She had a new accent that I couldn't quite place, but it screamed money.

There was no way anybody could buy such a grand story, but the clerk was eating it up.

"Well, of course," the woman said as she leaned in like she understood the perils of private planes. "We have the city's best dog hotel, with daily spa treatments, exercise classes, and all-organic food, which is prepared in-house by our chef de cuisine."

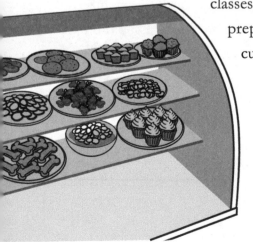

You have got to be kidding me.

"We're very particular about the kind of food Peaches eats. Would we be able to bring in our own food?"

"But of course."

"Excellent." Shelby gave the woman the most innocent of smiles. "I'd love a tour."

"It would be my pleasure. Please follow me." The woman held out her hand for Shelby to follow.

"Oh, and this is my basketball tutor, *Sherlock*." Shelby turned to face me and stuck out her tongue, which was completely out of character for both Shelby Holmes and Petunia Cumberbatch.

I bit the inside of my cheek so I wouldn't start laughing and blow our cover.

The woman opened a set of double doors, and I did my best not to cry out in protest. The hallway had rooms on either side that were about as big as my bedroom back home. Each one was for a dog.

Again. FOR. A. DOG.

Every room was brightly decorated with paint, photos of dogs, a bed, and toys. There were waist-high gates attached to each entry. The hallway then led to a play area, which looked more like a playground from when I was a kid, with slides, swings, and a running lane on the outside.

"This floor is for the smaller breeds. What kind of dog is Peaches?" the woman asked Shelby.

"She's a Cavalier King Charles spaniel. Do you have any of those here at the moment?"

"We indeed have two King Charles dogs currently boarding with us," the woman replied as she led us down another hallway with rooms.

Bingo!

Maybe one of the dogs was Daisy? Imagine how foolish Zane would end up feeling when he discovered that he was so close to Daisy when he was in here.

I felt my pulse begin to race as we were led to the first dog, who was called Lucky. While I'd never met Daisy, I knew that she had some brown fur on her face. This dog only had black-and-white fur.

I turned around to where the other King Charles dog was sleeping. All my hope was dashed when I noticed it was an older dog named Buzz. He lifted his head off the pillow he was resting on long enough to consider me, but then went back to sleep.

Daisy wasn't there.

I was waiting for Shelby to put this charade abruptly to an end, but she was on her knees petting Lucky and asking about boarding options.

I zoned out after I heard the woman excitedly describe their doggy pool, which was shaped like a bone.

The dog show was tomorrow. Each time it felt like we had a lead, we always seemed to take a step back.

We were being guided back to the front of the store.

Shelby took a brochure and patiently listened to the woman's final pitch.

"Sounds *wonderful*," Shelby said in her affected accent. "Daddy's personal attaché will be in touch to reserve a suite soon."

I was getting ready to head out the door, but Shelby wasn't done yet.

"Do you have any dogs competing in the Manhattan Kennel Club competition tomorrow? I hear that you're the preferred pet store for Daisy from the Upper West Side Lacys."

Was this something that I was going to have to do? Start referring to myself as John Watson from the Harlem Watsons?

"Oh yes," the woman chimed in excitedly. "We simply love Tamra and Zareen. It's a shame Daisy has gone missing." She gestured to the flyer that was up behind the counter.

"Oh, that is horrible!" Shelby held her hand up to her chest, like she was in shock.

Even though I knew Shelby was more than aware of Daisy's predicament, I almost believed how upset she was acting. She really was a good actress (as long as she didn't have to play the role of a friend . . . or a basketball player).

"And wasn't that Zane Lacy I saw on my way in?" Shelby batted her eyelashes.

The woman returned a blank stare. "I don't believe so. At least I didn't see him."

I did another sweep of the store. It was an open space and she would've definitely seen him when he was here. There was only one other customer when we walked in, and the guy behind the bakery counter was helping him and his black lab.

She had to have seen Zane.

Why would the woman lie about Zane being there?

Maybe *she* was the one who'd taken Daisy?

(I realized that I was grasping at straws, but time was ticking. The show was tomorrow and we had no other leads.)

She continued, "Then again, I haven't had the privilege of meeting Zane, but I've had the utter delight of getting to know his sisters and their fabulous dogs."

"Why, thank you so much," Shelby purred. "I do declare that you've been ever so helpful."

I didn't think it was possible for me to be more confused than when we left the store. But Shelby was elated.

"Watson!" she exclaimed. "We did it! Or rather, I should say, *I* did it. Oh, Tamra will be so pleased. Now I must determine the best way to do my reveal. I do think a little theatrics would be fun, don't you agree?"

"What?" I scratched my head, hoping that would get some blood flowing, because I had no idea what Shelby was talking about. What did she do? Daisy wasn't there.

"Oh, Watson." Shelby hit my arm, and it stung. She really was stronger than she looked. "The answer was literally right under your nose."

It was?

"What did I tell you?" Shelby wagged her finger at me like a teacher scolding a student (which was basically what she was doing). "Don't just *see*? You need to *observe*."

What had I missed?

ᴄ·CHAPTER·ᴐ
26

I WAS HOPELESS. AND UTTERLY CLUELESS.

I kept trying to put all the pieces together, but I couldn't. Shelby, in an attempt to either be as dramatic as possible or make me feel as stupid as possible (it was a toss-up), wouldn't tell me *what* exactly was under my nose.

I saw the two dogs that were Daisy's breed—one was too old, the other the wrong color.

What didn't I see?

"What should we do this weekend?" Mom asked expectantly as she dished out salad for dinner. "We can go downtown and see the Statue of Liberty or go to the Museum of Natural History. The city is ours."

I felt bad because I should spend Mom's first free day with her, but I'd been given explicit orders from Shelby that I was to report to the dog show with Sir Arthur at precisely nine o'clock tomorrow morning. She even gave me a map and detailed, step-by-step instructions on how to get there

(for which I was grateful but would never tell her that). As much as I was confused about my role in the case, and with Shelby in general, I had to find out who took Daisy.

"I wanted to check out that dog show tomorrow." I said it so casually, hoping she wouldn't be able to see through it.

"Really? I didn't think you were into dogs."

"Well, it's something different, and I thought . . ." I didn't want to lie to Mom, but I also knew she didn't want me to get involved in Shelby's cases.

"Maybe I should join you?" she offered. When I could only respond by stabbing a piece of kale, she arched her eyebrow. "John?"

"Shelby asked me to help her with Sir Arthur tomorrow. I need to take him to the show."

"Why?"

If only I knew the answer to that question.

"Does this have to do with a case?" She leaned back in her chair, a serious look on her face.

"No. I don't think so. Maybe." Although taking Sir Arthur to the dog show was all about the case. Everything about Shelby was about the case. "I guess."

"What did I say about getting involved in other people's business?"

"I know. It's just that I'm learning a lot from Shelby. You've seen what she does and she's so close to cracking this case. I want to see how it all plays out. Plus, I met Zane and all those other guys I played ball with today through her. So I feel like I owe her this one favor." I spoke so fast, hoping she wouldn't have a chance to argue.

"Does it really mean that much to you?"

"Yes." It did. It might have seemed like a silly thing, but I liked doing something so completely different from anything

I'd ever done before. So much had already changed for me. It was nice there was something that hadn't reminded me of how much I'd lost. "All I'm doing is taking Sir Arthur to the hotel. That's it." At least that was what I thought was it. I had no idea what tomorrow held. And it really excited me. It was a new adventure. "Please." The desperation in my voice was clear.

Mom studied me for a few more minutes before she finally spoke. "You can go to the dog show tomorrow, on two conditions."

"Okay," I replied hesitantly, wondering what her conditions could be.

"One, you have to do the dishes tonight and all next week." I nodded. I always had to rinse the dishes and put them in the dishwasher back at our old house, so this wasn't anything different. "And two, you have to spend Sunday with me."

"Deal!" I replied happily.

Mom laughed while she shook her head. "Please be careful. Shelby may be smart, but I'm not sure if she's a good influence on you."

Well, I couldn't really argue with her about that. Although I had a feeling if I ever talked to Mom the way Shelby seemed to talk to, oh, *everybody*, she'd quickly straighten me out.

"Oh, and, John," she said as she took her plate over to the sink. "We don't have a dishwasher in this apartment. Enjoy scrubbing!"

Aw man! I'd forgotten that. I looked over at the pile of dishes that were waiting for me.

First Shelby, and now my mom. Was there anybody who couldn't outsmart me?

CHAPTER 27

IF THERE WAS ONE THING I WAS GOOD AT, IT WAS FOLLOWING instructions.

Even as far back as kindergarten, I'd been praised for being a good listener and direction follower. Maybe that's from growing up in a military family, where discipline was a daily practice. Every post had different rules, so I'd become accustomed to reading lists and following them to a T.

So at precisely eight the following morning, I knocked on Mrs. Hudson's door so she could let me into the Holmes's apartment to get Sir Arthur.

"How's everything going so far?" Mrs. Hudson asked as she began unlocking the top lock.

"Pretty good," I replied, because how today played out was going to be a huge factor in how the rest of my week (if not my life here) was going to go. Depending on how Shelby handled the revelation of who took Daisy (along with the when, where, how, and why), either I'd have Zane as a friend or I wouldn't. Shelby didn't concern herself with people's feelings, so I was a nervous wreck that she was going to say something to make Zareen, Tamra, and/or Zane mad. Although it was pretty clear whoever did it was involved with the pet store, since Shelby had figured everything out when we were there. Or the Lacys could be so grateful to Shelby that I'd get bonus points for being involved.

Sir Arthur was waiting by the door. I attached his leash, grabbed the oversized canvas tote, and went back into the hallway.

Mrs. Hudson gave me a hopeful smile. "It's so lovely to see Shelby making a friend."

I wanted to ask her if Shelby made her "friends" schlep her dog downtown with an errand list in hand.

"Good luck with your case!" she called after me as I opened the front door.

Yeah, I had a feeling we were going to need all the luck in the world.

Sir Arthur and I made our way down the stairs and onto the sidewalk. I had studied the street map so closely that I was happy that we made it to the subway entrance ahead of Shelby's painfully detailed schedule.

Shelby told me dogs were only allowed on the subway if they were contained, which was why she gave me a huge canvas bag. I kept Sir Arthur to my outside as we went down the stairs. Luckily, the attendant in the booth wasn't paying attention, so I was able to slip Sir Arthur through undetected until we got to the platform. I laid out the canvas bag for him to crawl into. *He'll know what to do,* Shelby had told me.

Sir Arthur simply stared up at me, his tongue hanging out on one side.

"You're supposed to go in here!" I spread out the bag even wider.

He sat, his droopy eyes cast down at the bag, then up to me.

"What?" I asked him. I looked at Shelby's list, which explicitly stated that if I spread out the bag, he'd climb in and then I could get him on the train.

I heard rumbling up ahead and knew our train was approaching. There was a chance I could get away with bringing him onto the train without the bag, but I didn't want to risk it. I was already going to have to pretend to be Sheldon Holmes when I arrived, and I wasn't in the mood to tempt fate further by breaking any more laws.

Sir Arthur put his nose down on the bag and moved the strap out of the way, then used his teeth to pull the bag out farther. After he was happy with the bag placement, he crawled in.

I picked up the straps as the train arrived in the station. The bag wouldn't budge. Sir Arthur probably weighed fifty pounds. How exactly was I supposed to pick him up and carry him? Although I had a feeling that Shelby would've managed just fine.

The doors to the train opened, and a few people side-stepped us to exit. I dragged the bag a couple inches before Sir Arthur managed to free himself. He picked up the bag in his teeth and marched into the subway car. He then placed the bag down on the floor and crawled back in.

Smart dog.

Like I should've expected anything else.

I checked the subway map at every station, not wanting to miss the stop. I debated what to do once we got to our destination but had a feeling Sir Arthur would help me out.

The train pulled into our stop, which was on the corner of the hotel where the dog show was being held. Sir Arthur hopped back out of the bag. Once he was safely on the platform, he paused for me to put on his leash.

Two young women approached as I fumbled with the leash. I was certain they were going to get me in trouble for not having Sir Arthur contained in his bag.

"Your dog is so cute! Can I pet him?" One girl kneeled down beside Sir Arthur, who happily slumped onto his back so he could get a belly rub.

I checked the time to make sure we were going to be okay. Luckily, Shelby had anticipated this. Her timeline "took into account unforeseen factors, including you getting lost despite my clear instructions and the more likely case of having to deal with Sir Arthur's many admirers."

The girls helped me hide Sir Arthur from the attendant as we made our way up into the already humid Saturday morning.

While I was turned around, it didn't take long for me to figure out which hotel I was looking for. All I had to do was follow the line of dogs and owners streaming into a hotel high-rise.

Once I entered the hotel lobby, it was chaos. Dogs jumping and barking at each other, while their owners stood in line getting agitated. I was on my way to the registration desk when I heard my name called out.

"John!"

The voice came from the Lacy clan—all of them, including their trainer, were looking very worried as they sat in the lobby, without a dog.

"Have you seen Shelby?" Tamra asked as she nervously twisted her hair.

"She'll be here, with Daisy," I assured her. Even though I didn't know the how or where she was retrieving Daisy, I knew better than to doubt Shelby.

"This is ridiculous," Zane said as he threw his hands up in the air. "How dare she get your hopes up!"

"Classic Holmes, overconfident as ever," a voice replied.

I turned around to see Detective Lestrade, wearing a casual blue dress without her badge in sight.

"Hello, Detective," I said as I could feel the sweat starting to form on my forehead. What if she noticed that I was under the name Sheldon Holmes? What had Shelby gotten me into? "I didn't realize you were going to be here."

A smile started to spread on her lips. "Yes, well, I wanted to get a front-row seat to Holmes's *big reveal.*" She said those last two words with a smirk. She was here because she wanted to see Shelby fail. It never even occurred to me that there was a chance she wouldn't find Daisy.

"Watson." Emerson approached me. "Shelby asked me yesterday afternoon before she left to give you this." He handed me an envelope with my name written on it.

It didn't make any sense. Shelby had seen me after she gave him that letter. She had even given me her own letter with instructions last night.

I tore open the envelope, assuming that it was the same list I already had. She was probably simply covering her bases.

Oh, how wrong I was.

Dear Watson,
    Thank you for bringing Sir Arthur safely to the hotel. I had every faith you'd be able to complete

your task successfully. I must admit that I haven't been fully up front with you on what I require of you today. I will need you to be Sir Arthur's handler at the dog show. Simply make sure he has seen at least one dog compete and he'll know what to do. He's a very intuitive dog and he should be able to guide you expertly.

Shelby Holmes

She tricked me! There was no way I would've come here if I knew I had to be a dog handler. I was going to make such a fool out of myself. I glanced back down at the letter and noticed a postscript on the back.

PS—While I didn't want to deceive you, I knew this omission on my part was the only way to get you to do it. You won't make a fool out of yourself, as I've asked Mr. Emerson to assist you.

I looked around the hotel lobby, positive that I was going to see Shelby laughing. This had to be a prank. How did she know that was going to be my response?

Although of course she'd know how I'd react. This was her plan all along. She knew before she ran into me yesterday that she was going to have me do this. She knew when we were tailing Zane how everything was going to play out.

"Come along." Emerson gestured with his hand for me to follow him.

"Where are we going?" I asked, my head still spinning with the fact that I had to go onstage with Sir Arthur. Or at least I thought that was what I had to do, since I'd never even seen a dog show before.

I knew nothing.

And Shelby was throwing me to the hounds.

Emerson began to explain. "Since Sir Arthur has never shown before, he has to compete in the English bulldog preliminaries. If he places in the top two, then he goes to the Non-Sporting competition, much to Shelby's objections. She felt her dog was a rather sporting animal, but I don't make up the designations. This is where he'll compete against other dogs for a spot in Best in Show. If Shelby comes through, Daisy will compete right after Sporting in the Toy competition." He checked his watch. "She has a little over an hour to get here. You, on the other hand, have ten minutes."

WHAT!

Before I could really understand what was happening, Emerson led me up the escalators as he placed an armband with a number on my left arm.

He was telling me what to do during the show, but all I could think of was, *I have to show Sir Arthur.*

Or, as Shelby made it clear, it was more that Sir Arthur would be showing me.

I was getting used to playing second fiddle to Shelby, but couldn't I even get top billing over a dog?

CHAPTER
28

"Now, pay attention."

While I said that to Sir Arthur as we watched the competition from behind a heavy blue curtain backstage, I was also talking to myself.

It seemed pretty straightforward. I had to jog around an oval once with Sir Arthur and the other dogs, then a judge would check him out before we had to run back and forth the length of the floor.

How hard could it be?

But then again, there were probably around two hundred people seated on the outskirts of the oval course, including Detective Lestrade. Plus, Sir Arthur wasn't prepared. I had no idea the last time he'd been groomed. The judges were really going over the dogs: feeling their coat from every angle, examining their ears and tail, pulling apart their lips to check their teeth and gums, and lifting their feet.

Emerson took out a brush and worked through Sir

Arthur's coat. "He's a fairly clean dog," he remarked. "I usually make it a policy not to work with English bulldogs. They are tough to train, an extremely stubborn creature."

Hmmm. Remind you of anybody?

He took out a cloth and started cleaning Sir Arthur's folds.

Emerson sighed. "If I had more time with him, I could guarantee that he'd at least place. Why did Shelby want you to do this?"

To humiliate me was the first thought that popped into my head.

But she had wanted access to the backstage area where all of Daisy's competition was. *That* was why she had registered Sir Arthur.

Yet Shelby was nowhere to be found, and it didn't appear Daisy was here, either.

"Fortunately, handlers are supposed to be invisible," Emerson said as he looked down at my shorts and T-shirt with a disapproving shake of his head. "Are you ready?"

Yeah, Sir Arthur was the only one who was going to be judged.

Had I been clued into the fact that I'd be showing off a dog, I would've dressed better. Most of the other handlers had suits on. All the guys had ties. They were also at least twenty years older than me. *No*, I wasn't ready, but it didn't really matter, did it?

"One last adjustment," Emerson said as he pulled out a black-and-white-striped tie and adjusted it around my neck. "Shelby insisted."

Of course she did.

I stood in line and watched with a lump in my throat as the woman in front of me started running with her bulldog like wolves were chasing them.

I knelt next to Sir Arthur. "Okay, I'll try not to trip if you can promise not to bark or bite. You only have to look cute."

Sir Arthur replied by licking my face.

"Ah, maybe you aren't supposed to lick, either?"

The chief steward motioned for us to go.

"Here goes nothing," I said under my breath, then proceeded to trip over the carpet. Luckily, it was before we were officially on the course, but Sir Arthur looked up, and I swore he rolled his eyes at me.

We both took off and ran around the circle. I'd been told this was part of the agility test, to see the dog's willingness to work with the handler. We then stopped in the designated spot, where the judge approached us and had me turn Sir Arthur a few times on his leash. Well, I really didn't do anything, as Sir Arthur turned on his own.

The judge, an older woman with a fierce stare, pointed to the place where I was to stop with Sir Arthur. I mimicked the other handlers and knelt beside him. Everybody else had treats or a toy to keep the dog's head level while they were being judged. Emerson had told me that he mentioned this to Shelby, who objected to the treats, as it was "demoralizing" for Sir Arthur to be bribed.

"How old is he?" the judge asked as she knelt down next to Sir Arthur.

"Ah, he, ah . . ." I stuttered. I had no idea how old Sir Arthur was. You'd think with all that preparation, Shelby would've told me that one simple fact.

Sure, how dare *Sir Arthur* be the one to be demoralized, while I was doing fine on my own.

The judge looked up at me while I stood there with my mouth wide open. She must've seen the terror in my eyes, and returned to poking and prodding Sir Arthur. Sir Arthur didn't seem bothered by it all, while I could hardly breathe. Before I knew it, she was on to the dog next to us.

We were then instructed to run around one more time as a group. I kept looking at my feet, willing them to keep up and not trip. I doubt I was out there for more than five minutes, but it felt like an eternity.

The judge instructed us to go back to our designated posts, where the dogs were given one final look. She walked around a few times, being very careful and deliberate with her ranking.

I stared her down, almost willing her to place Sir Arthur.

What was I thinking? If he placed, I had to do this again.

No way. Shelby would be here any minute. She'd promised the Lacys. She wouldn't do that to me. Well, she wouldn't do that to me *again*.

The judge picked a black-and-white bulldog for first place. Then I could hardly believe it as she walked over to me. I'm sure I must've looked like I was in shock as she declared us, well, Sir Arthur as second place. There was an extra spring in my step as we did a celebratory lap.

"We did it!" I dropped down to my knees and hugged Sir Arthur.

Now I got why people did things like this—it was kind of like playing a sport. You got a total rush of adrenaline.

Sir Arthur and I jogged backstage, where we were greeted with congratulations from fellow competitors. The Lacys gave us a polite round of applause, although their mood had gotten worse since we were less than thirty minutes away from the Toy competition.

"Thanks," I replied, feeling guilty for showing off a dog that wasn't even my own.

"Yes, *Sheldon*, that was great," Lestrade said with a raised eyebrow.

The joy I felt was replaced with panic. Mom was going to kill me when I called her from jail. Because that was what happened when you lie about your name, right?

Before I could stammer out a reply, Tamra's eyes darted behind me, and she let out a joyous scream. "DAISY!"

We all turned around and saw Shelby walking triumphantly with a King Charles dog on a leash. But . . .

Even though Tamra was on the floor hugging the dog, whose tail was wagging so fast I expected it to fly off, the dog wasn't Daisy. It was the dog we saw at Pawesome Pooches. The one that was a different color.

It couldn't have been Daisy.

Could it?

CHAPTER 29

"What on earth?" Mrs. Lacy ran over to Tamra and the dog.

"You found her!" Tamra had her arms around the pooch. "I'm so sorry I doubted you."

Shelby shrugged. "Wouldn't be the first time I was underestimated." She was looking at Detective Lestrade when she spoke.

"But . . ." Mrs. Lacy looked between the dog and Shelby. "*Is* that Daisy?"

Thank you! I thought, glad not to be the only one who was confused.

"It is," Shelby replied confidently. "She'd been disguised."

All the Lacys were now gathered around the reunion. I stole a glance at Zareen, whose skin had turned to an ashen color.

No. She looked guilty. It was Zareen after all. I couldn't believe that I had fallen for her lies. I let her convince me she was innocent, even though she had the biggest motive of all.

"Please explain to me how you found her and who did this," Mrs. Lacy demanded.

"Of course." Shelby had a glow about her. I think this was her favorite part: when she got to fill us in on how brilliant she was (and how clueless the rest of us were). "Unless you'd like to."

We all looked around wondering who she was addressing. Obviously the guilty person would be able to explain exactly how they pulled it off, but WHO DID IT?

I looked at Zareen, who appeared utterly dumbfounded. But then there was a flash right next to her as Zane bolted toward the exit. Shelby stuck out her leg swiftly to trip him, as if she'd been anticipating it. Zane went sliding on the marble floor. Shelby grabbed his hand, and she put a handcuff around his wrist, then placed the other around hers.

Of course she had handcuffs. Of course *she did.*

"Zane?" Mr. Lacy said in a scolding voice. "What did you do?"

I felt sick as I waited for Zane to reply. There had to have been some mistake.

Zane, who had been so cool, nearly stoic, began to pout like a small kid. "I did it because I'm so sick of Zareen being treated like a second-class citizen in her own home. All you guys do is talk about Tamra and that stupid dog. Nothing Zareen does is good enough. I thought if Daisy skipped a show, we could return to normal."

Wait. My mind started to remember Zane saying something similar to me yesterday. But I disregarded it. Because I didn't want to believe that he could've possibly been responsible.

But he was.

"Zane"—Zareen sat on the floor next to her twin—"you did that for me?" She looked touched, before she hit him on the head. "You knew how much I was being blamed for it and you didn't say anything! How could you?"

"I'm sorry! I know! I didn't know what to do! I was planning on getting Daisy this afternoon and bringing her home. I was going to say she was wandering around or something. I didn't think it was going to be such a big deal. Why did you have to call them?"

To my horror, Zane pointed to Shelby and me with malice.

So my worst fear was confirmed: I was going to be exiled by association. Zane, who I thought was my friend, turned out to be a dognapper.

Mr. Lacy stood over his son. "We need to go have a talk." He looked down at Shelby, who seemed thrilled to be in the middle of a family breakdown. "Shelby, would you mind uncuffing my son so he and I can have a talk."

Shelby reluctantly took out the key and freed Zane.

Mr. Lacy took him by the collar and led him off.

Mrs. Lacy kept looking between everybody. "Okay, I know why Zane did it, but how?"

"I'm so glad you asked!" Shelby jumped up from the floor. "Unless you'd like to fill everybody in, *Detective*?"

Shelby locked eyes with Lestrade. Both of them had their arms folded. It seemed like years before Lestrade sighed heavily and walked away, muttering under her breath.

"What an absolutely delightful day!" Shelby declared.

"But *how*?" Mrs. Lacy reminded Shelby that the rest of us were still clueless.

"Yes!" Shelby was beaming. "Zane's plan was simple: take Daisy in the early morning and then stow her for a couple days at Pawesome Pooches. His first problem was ensuring that Daisy wouldn't be recognized. He used blackberries to dye Daisy's brown fur. I noticed the stain on his fingernails the other day, along with white dog hair on his shorts. I also had observed some of the dye in the corner of his bathtub when I took a closer look at the living quarters yesterday. Zane had never been in the store before, so he used a fake name to keep 'Lucky' there. What he didn't plan on was that Zareen would sleepwalk the night of the crime. She broke the frame, which he cleaned up because he didn't want her to be accused of taking Daisy. However, he missed a piece that was hidden under the bureau. He was able to escape with Daisy because he had put her in a large duffel bag to hide her from the cameras. Upon inspecting the footage, I found it odd that Zane had an extremely large bag that was moving. While he went under the guise that he was playing the basketball, he had flip-flops on. Watson had informed me not only that Zane had missed a game with his friends this week, but also that it would be quite difficult to play in flip-flops. Zane was the one who brought the food to Daisy, and I was able to confirm that he was supposed to pick her up later today. So he did plan on returning her. A simple case of sibling rivalry."

Mrs. Lacy stood there with her mouth open. "But kids can't board a dog without an adult."

I glanced at Emerson, knowing that this was probably his role in all this.

"Yes." Shelby nodded. "It needs to be someone at least eighteen years old and with a credit card. Watson?"

Why was she looking at me? I wasn't eighteen. I didn't have a credit card.

She continued, "It was the one piece that I couldn't quite figure out until I spoke to Watson yesterday afternoon."

Me? How did I help her out if I had no idea what she was talking about?

"Think, Watson," Shelby encouraged me. "You gave me

quite the detailed description of your game of the basketball yesterday, which was how I knew Zane missed a game sometime this week."

I told her that? Then I remembered the trash-talking that happened when Zane missed a basket. I thought they were just teasing each other. I didn't realize it was a clue.

Plus, I didn't think Shelby was even listening to me when I reenacted all the teasing. What else did I tell her? What else did I hear?

Flashes from yesterday started popping up in my head. A comment here and there. It all started to make sense.

"Corey!" I exclaimed. "He's eighteen. He mentioned something about Zane buying him shoes."

"Exactly," Shelby said with pride. "He signed the dog in, gave them the papers, and put it on a credit card. Thank you, Watson."

I felt like I was in a haze. All the evidence was placed in front of me, but I was too naive to see it. I didn't want to believe that any of the Lacys were guilty, especially Zane.

Since I was part of the team that caught him, there'd be no way he'd want to be my friend now. He wouldn't be able to trust me again after I got him in trouble.

Well, then maybe he shouldn't have stolen a dog.

Still, it stung. I liked hanging with him and his friends yesterday. He was the only friend I had made since I got here. Well, I thought he was my only friend since I still didn't know where things stood with Shelby.

Shelby seemed quite pleased with herself. "Oh, and, Mrs. Lacy, you should be aware that your son has a tell."

"A what?" She looked like she was in shock.

"Whenever he lies, he puts his hands in his pockets. I noticed it the other day when I was interrogating him."

Wait. So Shelby wasn't flirting with Zane after all. She was asking him all those random questions because she was trying to see what he was lying about.

Yeah, that made more sense. Shelby didn't seem like the type to be interested in guys. She didn't want friends—there was no way she'd be interested in a boyfriend.

This also meant that Shelby knew Zane was the lead suspect way before she trailed him. That was why she wanted me to play basketball with him. It wasn't to get rid of me (necessarily); it was to get intel. So I was useful after all!

John Watson: detective, truth seeker, and expert dog handler.

"I can't believe he did this to poor Daisy!" Tamra shouted, her grip tight around her dog's neck. She looked over at her older sister, who still appeared to be in shock. "I'm so sorry I thought you did it, Zareen."

Zareen gave a little nod, seeming to be confused over the turn of events.

See, I knew Zareen was innocent. So yeah, I totally didn't know who did it, but at least I was right about Zareen.

Tamra kept petting Daisy. "Can we even show her like this?"

Emerson dug through his giant leather bag for tools to see if Daisy's fur could be saved.

Mrs. Lacy finally snapped out of her fog. "Thank you so much, Shelby. What can we do to repay you for helping our family?"

Shelby's entire demeanor perked up. "I'd appreciate a pan of Miss Eugenia's walnut-fudge brownies." Shelby then turned to me. "And I must acknowledge Watson's role in all this."

As much as it pained me that this whole ordeal cost me Zane's friendship, I really appreciated that Shelby was acknowledging my help. I was a huge part of her figuring everything out, even if I had no clue I was doing it.

Shelby continued, "Would it be possible for Miss Eugenia to make him a batch of sugar-free brownies?"

"Absolutely." Mrs. Lacy gave me a kind smile. "I better go off . . ."

A team of groomers was around Daisy, combing and prepping her for her debut as a white- and raven-haired dog.

"Well, Watson, we did it!" Shelby declared with a slight nod in my direction.

Did she really use the word *we?* Maybe the great Shelby Holmes needed a partner (not an assistant) after all.

"Thanks for requesting brownies for me."

"You're welcome. And, Watson, thanks for helping me."

"Well . . ." I looked at Shelby, who was grinning from ear to ear. "That's what friends are for."

The word *friends* slipped out so naturally. While I was anticipating one of her patented grimaces, she perked up even further when I said it. "Really?"

"Well, yeah. Friends help friends."

"But you mean we're *friends?*"

While Shelby had seemed dismissive about having friends, I had a feeling the reason she thought she didn't need a friend was because she never really had one before.

What would being friends with Shelby Holmes mean? While I had no doubt that I'd be talked down to, even possibly made fun of by others, I had to say that being friends with her would be anything but boring.

"Yeah." I went to pat her shoulder, but she shrugged it away. "Friends."

"Friends," she replied with a nod.

I laughed. I never had to

declare my friendship with somebody before. Usually you hang out, keep hanging out, and you just become friends. But then again, I never had one like Shelby before.

We began walking around the backstage area, looking at all the dogs competing. "But how did you know that the dog at Pawesome Pooches was Daisy?"

"Well, I was aware that Zane had dyed Daisy's fur, so I knew what to look for. Plus, the biggest clue of all: the stuffed bone was in the room with her."

It *was* right under my nose, but I didn't know what to look for.

At that moment, a line of hound dogs came from the stage. I couldn't help but laugh.

"Look at that." I pointed to a brown bloodhound that was more wrinkled than my great-grandma. "He kind of looks like a detective, huh? I bet if we dressed him up in, I don't know, an old cape and matching deerstalker cap, with a pipe, he'd look just like a detective." I was cracking myself up, but Shelby was not amused.

"Seriously, Watson?" she asked. "You think a *real* detective would wear a cap and smoke a pipe?" She shook her head and then shoved a lollipop in her mouth. "Preposterous!"

Okay, there was a good chance the majority of my teasing would come from Shelby, but I think I can handle it.

CHAPTER 30

THE NEXT AFTERNOON, I FOUND MYSELF SITTING BACK ON our front stoop, writing in my journal.

It was weird not to have a case to think about. I spent last night telling Mom all about our day. She surprised me by playing a voice mail Dad had left yesterday for me, apologizing for not calling. He promised we'd talk tonight. "I really miss you, John," he had said before he hung up. It wasn't the same as having him here, but it would have to be enough, for now.

I looked back at my journal and got back to reporting on yesterday. Daisy won the Toy division, while Sir Arthur didn't even place in the Non-Sporting group. That wasn't Sir Arthur's fault, but Shelby's. She decided to give the judge a taste of her own medicine and, after looking the judge up and down, said something that made the judge take a step back and disqualify Sir Arthur.

Poor dog.

Daisy didn't get Best in Show, which didn't seem to upset the Lacys, as they were simply happy to have their dog back. I'd been informed that Zane had been grounded "indefinitely," and since I never got any of his friends' information, it looked like I was back to square one in the friend department.

Well, except I'd already made one friend.

I heard the front door open behind me, and it unnerved me how excited I was to see Shelby standing over me.

"That was something yesterday," I remarked to her. "Although . . ." I hated that I went online this morning to see if anything had been written up about how we solved the case. "Did you see the article about the dog show and how Daisy was missing until right before showtime?"

"I don't bother with old news," Shelby said with a sniff as she continued down the stairs.

"But you didn't get mentioned." (Neither did I.) "It made it seem like she simply materialized out of thin air. You deserve more than baked goods for what you did. You should've gotten credit."

"What do you want me to do, Watson? Hire a publicist? Nobody will ever believe that a 'little girl' could do all that."

"Yeah, but . . ." I said as I looked down at my hands. I held up my journal. "I've begun writing everything down here. *I'll* tell your story."

Shelby tilted her head as she studied me. I knew her ego couldn't resist being written about. "Suit yourself."

She skipped down the steps.

"*Or*"—Shelby turned around with a crooked smile—"there's a case I've been called in on that may require your expertise."

"Like a partner?" I asked. While I knew that I couldn't hold a candle to Shelby's sleuthing, I could help her with dealing with normal people and things she didn't find to be "essential" enough to be in her brain attic.

"Yes, Watson. As my partner."

I quickly stashed my journal away. There'd be plenty of time for me to record our adventures. As Mom kept reminding me, I wasn't going anywhere.

"Hurry up, Watson!" Shelby called behind her back as she started walking down the street. "We've got another case to solve."

ACKNOWLEDGMENTS

Unlike Shelby, I have no trouble asking for help. I'm fortunate to have such wonderful people in my life who offered endless advice and encouragement while I was writing this book.

Everybody at Bloomsbury has been welcoming and supportive of Watson, Shelby, and me since day one. Huge thanks to my editor, Catherine Onder, and Hali Baumstein for their thoughtful notes; Diane Aronson and Nancy Seitz for reigning in the Queen of Split Infinitives; and the whole Bloosmbury crew, especially Cindy Loh, Cristina Gilbert, Lizzy Mason, Melissa Kavonic, Jessie Gang, Erica Barmash, Beth Eller, Emily Klopfer, and the sales department.

I've never had character illustrations before, and I'm so honored to have Erwin Madrid bring Watson and Shelby to life.

I can't begin to express how lucky I am to have such a fabulous team at WME represent me. I could never thank Erin Malone enough for encouraging me to write this book solely from a one-sentence description. Also, I'm grateful to Laura Bonner for helping Watson and Shelby take over the world!

Jen Calonita is not only my author-tour bestie, she took time off from working on her own books to read a rough draft and offered such wonderful advice. Our next round of cupcakes is on me!

Fun fact: I am nowhere near as smart as Shelby. So I had to do a lot of research for this book. Colonel Erica Nelson, U.S. Army, spent time answering my questions about army-post living (special shout-out to my brother-in-law, Mark Vodak, for the hookup, and Erica's daughter Briana for being such a great reader!). I'm also grateful to Tiffani Diggs for letting me harass her on Facebook with questions about army posts. Julia Thorpe was so sweet to help a stranger with questions about having diabetes as a kid.

I don't think there's an author I have crossed paths with in the last two years whom I haven't talked to about this book and sought advice from. Thank you to Coe Booth, Sarah Rees Brennan, Ally Carter, Julia Devillers, Varian Johnson, David Levithan, Sarah Mlynowski, Marie Rutkoski, Carrie Ryan, Kieran Scott, Jennifer E. Smith, and (honorary author) Rose Brock.

Kirk Benshoff not only does a killer Kermit the Frog impression while singing "Rainbow Connection," he keeps my website in running order (and doesn't get mad when I go in and mess something up).

I'd be nothing without my family. They give me so much support and don't mind that I bring my laptop everywhere. Another fun fact: my brother, W.J., played Sherlock Holmes in a middle-school musical, while I was relegated to the chorus. May Shelby Holmes prove girls can solve crimes as well as the boys!

Of course, Shelby and Watson wouldn't exist without the original Sir Arthur. For decades, Sir Arthur Conan Doyle has inspired many with his stories featuring Sherlock Holmes and Dr. John Watson, including yours truly (as if it weren't obvious!). Believe me, as someone who is a huge fan of English bulldogs, naming a dog after him is a compliment!

SHELBY AND WATSON HAVE ANOTHER CASE TO SOLVE . . .

Read on for an excerpt from the second book
in the Great Shelby Holmes series.

You'd think having a friend who's a know-it-all would be annoying. And okay, at times it really, really is. *But* it can also be fascinating. And extremely helpful.

Especially if it's your first day at a new school.

"I see Sasha's parents didn't take her to Greece like they promised," Shelby remarked as we walked down the hallway at the Harlem Academy of the Arts. I followed her gaze to a white girl with her blond hair in a ponytail. There was absolutely nothing about this girl that would've led a normal person to think that Sasha didn't go on some family vacation.

But while Shelby Holmes was many things, normal wasn't one of them.

"How did you—" I began to ask before she cut me off.

"Like it isn't obvious," she replied with a huff.

A teacher standing outside a classroom looked up from a

folder. As soon as he saw Shelby, he quickly turned around, went into his classroom, and closed the door.

The only thing that seemed obvious to me was that there was a path being cleared for Shelby as we walked. I'd learned a few things from Shelby in the three weeks I'd known her. One was to make deductions based on people's behavior. Right now, I was deducing that nobody in the school wanted Shelby to do that thing she did.

Me included.

I also learned to listen to everything she says. And that she's always right.

While she kept casually spilling the secrets of our classmates and teachers as we continued down the hall, I looked around my new school. From the outside, it looked like a standard school building: redbrick and nothing special. But as soon as we stepped inside, it was everything I'd hoped a charter school focused on the arts would be: the walls were covered with student artwork, music filled the halls, and there were tryout flyers up for the fall musical. There was even an entire glass display case filled with books. But they weren't regular books found in other schools. These were the yearly anthologies the Academy put out featuring the best student writing.

Someday I'll be in there, I hoped.

Yeah, I could totally get used to a place like this. I had

two classes where I got to focus on my writing. *Two!* *And* I was going to be staying here. No more moving for the Watsons. We were making New York City our home.

Of course that meant I really needed to make a good first impression, since I'd be sticking around. I was used to being the new kid. I mean, I'd spent all eleven years of my life moving from army post to army post. But this was my last day as the new kid at a new place. It was different.

Shelby grunted, which brought me back to her orientation of my new classmates. "Like it isn't abundantly apparent she got kicked out of camp this summer."

"Who are you talking about?" I glanced around the hallway.

"Watson," Shelby said with a disapproving shake of her head. "What have I been telling you about observing?"

"I have been observing, but it would help if you could tell me *how* you know these things. Or, you know, start with *who* you're even talking about." My eyes swept my fellow classmates to find a clue about anything having to do with *anyone* at this point. I kept observing the same things as Shelby, but could never see what she saw.

"Fine!" she said with a groan. Her hand flew up and pointed to three girls talking by a locker. "Do you see how two of the girls have matching homemade rope bracelets? Standard last-day-of-camp fare. Pretty uninspiring if you ask me. Charlotte's not only missing one, but notice the lack of color on her, unlike the other two."

Yeah, the two other girls were more tan or whatever, but that could mean anything. How on earth did Shelby come up with someone being kicked out of camp?

Okay, I technically know how she did it. By deductive reasoning. But that doesn't mean I fully understood it. What Shelby's been trying to teach me to do is to assemble a list of likely scenarios based on observations, and then decide which option fit best. In the case of these three girls, the only scenario I had was that just one of them used sunscreen.

Shelby took my silence as ignorance. "I had to listen to them blather on and on last year about their horseback riding camp. So the missing markers of attending said camp for an extended period were glaringly obvious on Charlotte."

But I wasn't here last year, so how could *I* have known?

"And no, you're not off the hook simply because you weren't here last year," Shelby said as if she had read my mind. Maybe she had. "What can you tell by their interaction? Look closely," she instructed me.

I studied the three girls. Hmmm . . . Now that Shelby pointed it out, the two tan girls were talking animatedly, moving around their hands, laughing and talking over each other. While the other girl shifted uncomfortably from foot to foot, giving a polite smile every once in a while. So she didn't know the story the others were telling. And appeared a little jealous of it.

Maybe Shelby was right. (Wait, there's no maybe. She *was* right.)

"Okay, one girl feels left out, but still . . ." I could only see things once Shelby pointed them out. It was hard for me to put two and two together with basically nothing.

Shelby continued to walk down the hallway, while I tried to come up with more deductions.

"Maybe she has an allergy and couldn't go?" I took a stab in the dark.

"She went the previous year. It was all she talked about at the beginning of fifth grade."

"Oh, so you're friends."

Shelby stopped and looked at me with her patented look of disgust and aggravation. It was a look I'd gotten used to pretty quickly. "Friends? Oh, please be serious, Watson."

I knew Shelby didn't really think friends were important, but was it such a ridiculous assumption? Shelby was familiar enough with this Charlotte person to know she went to camp every summer. That would've required a conversation, wouldn't it? Some friendly banter? She couldn't decipher everything about a person by simply observing.

"Freak!" someone shouted in the hallway to the snickers of a few students.

On the other hand . . . maybe Shelby really didn't have friends, since everybody at this school was aware of what she could do—most of her clients were her classmates—and seemed to want no part of her.

I don't know. I just assumed everybody at school would think that she was weird (because she was) but still be impressed by her. I'll admit that I thought she was just a freaky science geek when we met on my first day in our new apartment building. But once I got past her grumpy attitude, I respected her. Everybody in our Harlem neighborhood admires her for her abilities.

But instead, when Shelby walked by, shoulders tensed and voices lowered.

It didn't take a genius of Shelby's caliber to realize that she wasn't well liked at school.

And here I was, on my first day, walking down the hallway with her. So much for a great start.

Stop it, John. I reminded myself that Shelby had helped me a lot during my first few days in New York City. We were friends. (Okay, she was my *only* friend here.) Plus, we were partners.

Shelby stopped dead in her tracks to the unease of the students around us. She was staring at a teacher who was in the hallway greeting students.

"The new science teacher, Mr. Crosby," Shelby informed me, but there was an edge to her voice.

I ignored the stares from the kids around us as I waited for her to tell me about our teacher.

Shelby remained quiet, her eyes surveying Mr. Crosby. My guess was that she was building up tension, something she liked to do, for a dramatic reveal.

"Well?" I asked her, anxious to get to my first class.

Then Shelby Holmes, detective extraordinaire, said the three words I thought would never come out of her mouth.

"I don't know."

I'm not sure what worried me more: that there was something the great Shelby Holmes didn't know, or that she marched right up to the new teacher and dropped to the floor to start examining him from the shoes up.

"Excuse me?" Mr. Crosby asked the top of Shelby's red frizzy curls. "Can I help you with something?"

When Shelby didn't answer, Mr. Crosby looked at me.

Since this poor teacher was new, I guessed somebody needed to tell him that Shelby was just being . . . well, Shelby.

And that lucky person was me.

"Hi," I said with a friendly smile. "I'm John Watson. It's my first day here, too."

"Hello, John," Mr. Crosby replied as he moved his feet around in an effort to shake Shelby. Of course this only resulted in irritating her. "Nice to meet you."

"You, too. I just moved to the neighborhood from Maryland, near DC. My mom used to work in the military.

Now she's a doctor over at the Columbia University Medical Center." I don't know why I felt the need to give Mr. Crosby my life story, but I was trying to put him at ease while Shelby did her thing.

In the short time we'd been working together, this had become my role in our partnership. Although it had taken a while for Shelby to realize that she needed my help. She definitely had the smarts to solve cases on her own, but it was her people skills that needed some work.

"Yeah, this is—"

"Shelby Holmes," Mr. Crosby finished my sentence. "Yes, I've been . . . informed." I was pretty sure he'd been *warned*, but caught himself.

I attempted to do my own investigation of Mr. Crosby. He looked like your typical white guy teacher: blue button-down shirt, khaki pants, and brown loafers. He was probably in his late twenties. He had short brown hair, brown eyes, and an average height and build. Pretty standard. Nothing remarkable about him.

Maybe not everybody had some story that Shelby could decode by a smudge on their glasses or how they tied their shoes.

Could it be possible that Mr. Crosby was simply a regular, boring teacher?

Shelby finally stood up and narrowed her eyes at him.

"Hello, Shelby," Mr. Crosby said with a hesitant smile. "Did you find whatever you're looking for?"

Shelby's scowl confirmed that she, in fact, had not. "You taught at a private school before? No!" she screeched. "Don't tell me!"

Mr. Crosby's attention shifted again to me. "Why don't I make this easy for everybody: I taught at Miss Adler's School for Girls on the Upper East Side for—"

"Two years," Shelby interrupted him. "Yes, I'm not an imbecile."

Mr. Crosby's eyes grew wide. "How did you . . ."

Apparently he didn't take those warnings about Shelby seriously.

"It's just this thing she does." I repeated the line that I'd been told when I had first met Shelby. It was something I'd been forced to say a lot these last three weeks.

My attention drifted to a familiar face in the hallway. It took me a second to remember that I already knew one other person who goes to the Academy.

"Tamra!" I called out.

Tamra Lacy was walking down the hall with three other girls. Even though she had on the same maroon Harlem Academy of the Arts polo shirt that every student wore, it was clear from her appearance that Tamra had money. I mean, yeah, I already knew that from being at her family's insane mega-apartment that overlooked Central Park. (And having met her family's personal chef and maid and driver.) But it was more than that. It was the way her black patent leather shoes shone in contrast to the other girls' canvas shoes, and how neatly pressed her shirt was compared to the wrinkles the majority of us sported.

Maybe my deductive reasoning wasn't so shabby after all.

Yet there was one mystery I couldn't figure out: why Tamra didn't seem to hear me.

"Tamra!" I called out again. "Hey!"

Her dark brown eyes glanced sideways. "Hi, John," she said softly, almost like she was embarrassed. A couple of her friends were whispering while stealing glances at Shelby.

Interesting. Well, it wasn't interesting that Tamra's friends would treat Shelby like everybody else did. What didn't make sense was why Tamra was being so cold to us, especially since it was Shelby who found Tamra's missing dog.

Although Tamra wasn't the first Lacy to disappoint me. It turned out it was her brother Zane, the first (and so far only) non-Shelby friend I made in New York, who stole her dog. Not surprisingly, after I helped Shelby prove he was the culprit, Zane didn't want to be friends with me anymore.

"Excuse me, John?" Mr. Crosby was leaning against the wall, Shelby's eyes only inches from his shirt. "Do you think you could help me? It's about time you get to class."

"Oh, right!" I took Shelby's arm and led her away, despite her protests.

"Something's not right," Shelby said between clenched teeth.

"Or maybe he's just a regular dude. Not everybody's a criminal mastermind." I took out my schedule and double-checked what room I was going to.

"Next door on the left," Shelby remarked. "I'll be across the hall if you need me."

"Thanks! Have a good day, Shelby!" I went to open the classroom door, but found it was locked.

"Your other left, Watson," Shelby said with a grimace. "And one more thing."

I stopped, waiting for some words of wisdom from Shelby that would help me navigate this school, just like she had helped me get around my new neighborhood. Although school was where I could really shine: I was a decent student. I could make friends easily.

But Shelby was Shelby, and I'd take any advice from her I could get.

"There's something that teacher is hiding. Mark my words: I'm going to find out what."

Shelby's face was deadly serious.

Photo © Liz Ligon

Elizabeth Eulberg is not a detective (or so she claims). She is, however, the author of *The Great Shelby Holmes* and *The Great Shelby Holmes Meets Her Match*, as well as internationally bestselling young adult novels *The Lonely Hearts Club*, *Prom & Prejudice*, *Take a Bow*, *Revenge of the Girl with the Great Personality*, *Better Off Friends*, *We Can Work It Out*, and *Just Another Girl*. Elizabeth lives outside Manhattan, where she spends her free time stalking English bulldogs in her neighborhood and filling her brain attic with random pop-culture facts.

www.elizabetheulberg.com
Twitter: @ElizEulberg